DAYS ARE GONE

a novel by Alan Watt

writers tribe books

Published by Writers Tribe Books
www.writerstribebooks.com

Book design by Amy Inouye, Future Studio

Published in the United States of America

ISBN 978-1-937746-22-3

To Mary-Beth

1

Chick was on a jet home.

He left seven weeks ago to rock mid-sized auditoriums in Sweden and Japan, while Alice stayed home and stared at the orange bridge across the bay. She used binoculars, scanning the ledge for a jumper. She didn't want to see anyone die—she just wanted to see them jump.

She read in the paper about some guy who, the moment he leapt, realized he wanted to live.

And he did.

He got an agent and began working the circuit sharing his near-death experience to high-school students, along with a slide show of his bone-crushing injuries and a souvenir CD of his heavy metal music. He shouted at these kids to chase their dreams. "Stop sabotaging yourself with negative self-talk," he said. "You deserve greatness, and greatness deserves you." He explained how his leap transformed him, how he began jogging regularly and no longer huffed paint to cope with rejection. Colors looked brighter. Food had more flavor. He cried more easily, which was, in part, a by-product of the PTSD from his botched death jump. He forgave his parents and moved out of their attic. He cut his hair, stopped smoking, got his GED, lifted weights, showered regularly, went vegan, meditated transcendentally, deleted his porn collection, recycled, joined Costco, became a Big Brother, registered to vote, threw out his futon, installed drapes, signed his organ donor card, returned his library books, invested in Apple, made amends to his bass player for going solo, joined an Episcopalian ministry where he accepted Christ as his savior, learned Quicken, quit shoplifting, paid his taxes, bought a hybrid, fed the poor, cycled the AIDS ride, rescued a greyhound, volunteered at a battered women's shelter where he met his future wife, became stepfather to her three children, cut out sugar, and mostly stopped masturbating.

Alice hated this story. She wondered how many impressionable minds left his presentation believing the key to a better life began with a failed suicide.

*　*　*

Her phone rang. "Babe, I just landed," said Chick. "I don't have my keys. You at home?"

"I'm here," she said. She packed quickly.

She dropped her key into an envelope and taped it to the front door with a note: *Bye, Chick. I'm leaving.*

She'd practiced the letter for seven weeks, running sentences in her mind, but every word left her feeling open to ridicule, until the note was reduced to a single line.

And now, seeing it on paper, it didn't look right. But she was out of time.

At the bottom she wrote: *Sorry.*

And she fled.

2

She stepped onto the elevator. It fell twenty-six floors to the garage. She waited while the valet sprinted to her car, a silver Volvo she'd bought a year earlier for her thirty-sixth birthday, and drove it forty feet to where she stood.

She headed north to Seattle where she planned to stay with her folks. She needed time to adjust, to figure out her next step. As she drove, she played both sides of the conversation she would have with her mother: "Chick and I are taking some time apart."

"Why? What happened?"

Alice didn't have an answer, not one that would satisfy her mother. "Nothing happened. We just need a break."

"Are you leaving him?"

"God no! We just need some space."

"But I don't understand. Every time we talk you tell me how wonderful things are."

To which she would respond cryptically: "I think he's going through some stuff."

"What stuff?"

"I don't know," she would say, or maybe, "He's being very distant," which was technically not a lie, except she would pretend it was a recent thing.

After two weeks she would ease her parents into it: "We're just so different. I don't know why I married him."

"Are you thinking of getting a divorce?"

"That's not what I want," she would say, which was also sort of true, because no one does.

And after a month: "I can't go back. It's over."

She'd fought to be with him, but now she realized that her folks' original judgment was accurate. "He's a little strange," her father had said. This wasn't a minor mistake like bringing home a professional juggler. It was thirteen years of pretending to be in love. The years floated past and she fell into a contented torpor. It wasn't a bad marriage. They didn't fight or throw things. From the outside it looked ideal.

Aside from being nineteen years her senior, Chick liked to drink and take mood-altering substances. When her mother, Trish, first saw him on *The Tonight Show*, she'd asked, "Was he drunk? He looked high. Is he an alcoholic?"

Alice explained that he was sober now (not true), and that because he was an artist, people often confused his off-kilter perspective for substance abuse. This intrigued Trish and she embraced Chick's weirdness, hung on every random digression. "Oh Chick, you are something," she would say following some rant where he deconstructed the underlying tenets of American democracy as a model of fascist ingenuity designed to sublimate suburban outrage.

In fact, Trish felt a kinship with him, and although she could not articulate it, she related to the struggle of holding onto one's identity amidst loved ones who saw things differently, though she told Alice she just felt bad him.

Alice knew that if she waited for Chick to come home she wouldn't leave. She usually joined him on the road, but this time she wanted to be alone. It was never love. She wanted it to be, and for years convinced herself it was, because it would have been convenient. But it wasn't. Chick was a habit. He had a gravitational pull. And when she was around him, she wanted more. Being with him wasn't difficult—it was easy. Her job was to be cool. With her lanky frame, blonde tresses and delicate features she looked the part—the blue-eyed babe who knew how to hang, how to go with the flow, how to roll with it. She quickly adopted Chick's gift for being so ironic that no one understood what the hell she was talking about. Chick was calibrated to be fascinating in short bursts, and had mastered the art of self-mythologizing as deprecation: *"I don't deserve to be called a legend,"* he once told their dinner guest. His friends were famous, but he was the mysterious one, the bearded intellectual eschewing commercial success for a rarer brand of fame. He was the unflappable bard of indifference who made not giving a shit seem noble. His songs referenced Foucault and Galbraith. He made rhymes with words like *exigent, tribunal,* and *nomenclature,* and sang songs about genocide and his cock. When people talked about Chick Wolfson it was usually with a grin and a sense of awe. He was an original, a tormented musical genius who threw his gifts on the pyre of alternative rock, that indefinable subset catering mostly to sunken-chested college boys with torn vintage T-shirts and body odor; emotionally delayed fantasists who lionized Chick for his promise to never write a love song. Chick was the opposite of radio-friendly and had assured his place in history by selling fewer records than all of his contemporaries and having exactly one top-ten hit, "Alien

Love," a cynical goof he and his backup band knocked off in the studio one night, which became the song that defined him, that allowed him to pack three-thousand seat theaters for another decade and a half after its release and perpetuate his particular brand of literate, misanthropic, weed-fueled, vaguely paranoid, minor-chord rock.

She wished she'd called ahead and prepared her folks, but she didn't know until the moment she heard his voice on the phone whether or not she would leave. He was home by now, probably for hours, and had read her note. So why was he not calling? Her heater blasted but her fingers were icicles and her teeth clacked loudly. She drove in silence past thick redwoods that shot through the clouds. On her left, jagged rocks jutted into the surf. The sun fell through the ocean. The air grew cold. And then it was dark and there was nothing on the radio but fuzz.

She pulled into a Holiday Inn off the highway. "It's not accepting your card," said the night manager.

"Could you please try again?"

She handed him two more cards, but she already knew the outcome. Chick gave her an allowance, but he controlled the money. He was generous, and she never took advantage of it. She wanted him to know that he married well. It was his third try, and she was determined to love the cynic out of him. And now the son of a bitch had cut her off. She wanted to scream at him to fight for her, but he would just hang up. Chick never argued. Ever. He left the room and smoked a blunt. There was a jabbing pain in her ribs. She wondered, *what, precisely, is this arrangement we have?*

She reached into her purse and counted forty-seven dollars.

She needed money.

"Hello, Mom?"

"Alice? What time is it?"

"Eleven-thirty."

"What's wrong?"

"Nothing, I just wanted to . . ."

She couldn't do it. Everything would come out.

"Sorry, Mom, I misdialed, I was actually calling . . . never mind."

"Is everything okay?"

Her parents would not understand. They loved Chick for being the kind of husband who could provide a secure life for their daughter. Alice's father was a noted litigator, and when he got home retreated to his office with a tumbler of scotch while her mother read war novels in the parlor. In a way, her marriage was identical to theirs, which is why her reasons for leaving would either make no sense to them, or would hit too close to home.

"Everything's fine, Mom. Go back to sleep." She stared out the window. It was raining.

The night clerk said, "There's a place in Waiden, 'bout twelve miles inland. They got cheap rooms at the Frontier. Just head back a mile and go east."

Alice felt dizzy. She grabbed onto the counter.

"Ma'am, are you okay?"

She smiled. "I don't know."

"We can't give our rooms away. I wish we could."

"Of course not," she said. "Where am I anyway?"

"This is the Holiday Inn Express off route nine."

"No, like . . . I mean, where am I?"

"Oregon? Is that what you mean? You're in Oregon."

"Oregon," she said.

She ran outside, shielding her head from the rain. She

darted back to her car, repeating it to herself. Oregon. I'm in Oregon.

She climbed into her car and shut the door. Oregon. She laughed. I did it, she thought. She turned the key. Her tank was nearly empty. But she was free.

3

She headed inland through a dark tunnel of towering firs when her car was hit with a rank, sulfurous stench. A giant plywood sign read: WAIDEN FOREST PRODUCTS. The rain hit her windshield in steady plops. She drove for twelve miles until the road opened up to a cluster of buildings.

Downtown Waiden was four short streets built on an incline. Alice came to a stoplight. On her right was darkness. She lowered her passenger window and felt a blast of cold air and heard rushing water. In front of her, on the corner was a neon sign that read: FR TIER HO EL.

The Frontier Hotel was a squat, three-story building at the bottom of the hill; its parking lot a pot-holed maze. She pulled in slowly and shut off the engine. She sat in silence, her body vibrating from the drive, then climbed out of the car and dragged her suitcase to the front door.

She pushed open the door into a dim cavernous lobby with threadbare carpet. A man sat at a plywood desk, his eyes fixed on a small TV. He wore a T-shirt stretched tight across his enormous belly. His beard hung down to his chest.

"Hi. I need a room."

He kept his eyes on the TV. "By the night or the week?" His beard was so thick she could barely see his lips move.

"Just the night."

"Twenty-five cash," he said. His eyes were dull black stones.

She counted twenty-five dollars from her purse and laid it on the counter. He snapped up the money and counted it. His hands were enormous. He pulled a key from the plywood board. "Room six. Up the stairs and down the hall. Bathroom's door next to yours."

"I share it?"

"Ruth don't get home till two."

"Ruth. Well at least it's a girl, right?" she said.

He ignored her and went back to his fishing program.

She walked to the stairs. A man sat against the wall, his eyes followed her through two narrow slits. His teeth were rotten. His right arm ended at the elbow, a ruby stump poked out from his stained T-shirt.

Her bed was a thin mattress over a handmade plywood box. She removed her shoes and stepped on the floor. It was sticky. She put her shoes back on. She tried to lock the door but the latch stuck. When she twisted it, it didn't move.

She went into the hall. A door clicked open and she turned to see the man with rotting teeth standing inside his doorway. He pushed his knotted forehead against the doorframe. His shoulder worked vigorously. She followed his arm down to where his hand was lost inside his trousers.

She ran down the hall.

"I need a different room. The lock on my door is broken."

The man shook his head. "No more rooms."

"Then I need the lock fixed."

"Guy comes on Monday."

"What happens when a lock breaks on Tuesday? That guy in the room across from me—he's a fucking pervert."

"Percy lives here."

"I'm better off sleeping in my car."

The man took her key and put it back on the nail. He opened his drawer and placed her money on the counter.

She watched the rain pound the window. "Will you be here all night?"

"Till four, anyway."

"What time does that creep fall asleep?"

The man's beard moved slightly, like he was smiling. "You'll be all right."

"Don't let me die."

The linoleum floor in her bathroom curled at the corners. The grout was lined with mold. On a shelf above the toilet was a lady's compact of glitter makeup. Alice washed her face with a sliver of soap, and then brushed her teeth. As she stepped into the hall a door opened and Percy watched her rush back to her room. She tried to move the bed frame but it was nailed to the floor. She pulled the mattress off it and slid it against the door.

She lay there, listening for sounds. A spring poked her ribs. She turned and it followed her like a phantom knuckle. Footsteps moved down the hallway. She could hear men's voices outside her door. She pressed her hand against the door, and after a few minutes they said goodnight.

Later, she heard more footsteps and the sound of a woman's voice. "Percy, close that door or I will rip that thing from its root!" It was a strange voice, smoke-ravaged, broken, pulsating with life. The door shut next to her and a moment later she heard the opening chords of Bob Dylan's "Tangled

Up in Blue." And then that voice—singing loudly to the stereo. By the end of the song Alice was wide-awake. She watched the rain hammer the window. She sat with her back against the door and waited for morning.

4

The ringing of tap water hitting aluminum disturbed the early morning quiet of his apartment—*efficiency suite* was how it was described to him by Waiden's lone parole officer: a single room, beige walls, with a shower and a hot plate. Webb Cooley placed the pot on the stove. He did military pushups, elbows tucked at his ribs, counting to a hundred before falling to the floor and gulping for air. It felt good, hot skin against cold wood. He ignored the sharp pains that shot through his hands. He balled them tight into fists, and then fanned the fingers to regain circulation. His knuckles ached. In the past few weeks pin-sized lesions appeared at the tips of his fingers.

He went to his bathroom, a tight square with a toilet and shower. Since being released from Oregon State Correctional Facility eight months earlier urinating was hell. He had worked in the kitchen and was required to ask permission before using the toilet, and now, after twenty years of institutional living, pissing required concentration.

"Permission to use the head sir," he whispered.

"Permission granted," he replied. And then, slowly at first, he began to piss, a weak, uncertain stream.

He ate while gazing down at the neon sign across the street. It read: Pastime Tavern. It was where he used to drink before he was put away at the age of nineteen, and now, staring down at the ghosts of his past, it shocked him to see the same faces, twenty years on, still telling the same lies under the awning. It bugged him that the only lodging in his price range gave him full view of a place he'd spent twenty years trying to forget. In fact, he wished he could forget this whole town, or maybe just that its inhabitants could forget what he had done.

He pulled on canvas trousers and a wool sweater. He went to the door and stopped. He knelt at the edge of the bed, closed his eyes, interlocked his fingers and prayed for God to get him through the day.

It was still dark. The rain fell softly as he walked down the hill. A car approached. Two figures sat in the front seat. His chest tightened as he imagined what they might be saying about him. At the bottom of the hill he pulled the key from his pocket and opened the front door of the Waiden General Store, a long room with three aisles. Fruit was stacked in pyramids along the side windows, with sweet corn and the last of the melons sitting in low bins. Stretching half the length of the store on the south side was an old display case for fish. Waiden's General Store had the only selection of fresh fish in town; striped bass, lingcod and tuna, fresh off the commercial boats from the Port Orford fisheries.

Webb closed the door behind him and wiped his feet on the mat. He went to the stockroom for the broom and swept the floor before washing the insides of the windows. He took the key from his boss's desk drawer and went into the alley. He pushed the key into the iron-barred door of the back cellar and descended the weathered stone steps. He lugged boxes of soft drinks into the store, dropped them in front of the cooler, then returned to the cellar for more non-perishables.

He was restocking a shelf when he heard the squeal of his boss's brakes outside. He entered the alley as George climbed out of his pickup. "No more ocean salmon this year," said George, hobbling to the truck's rear. His cane stabbed the pavement. "Say it's overfished, shut down the coast for the rest of the season." His one good eye bulged, like he expected Webb to change the state's decision.

George wore a porkpie hat and red-checkered fishing jacket to keep the rain out. His left side hung limp from the effects of a stroke. He had wide hips and narrow shoulders and wore his crisp cotton shirt tucked tightly into a pair of high-riding khakis. His body was frail, his foot dragged when he walked, but he grinded on with a look of desperation shrouding his eyes, some inborn terror that he was forever on the brink of disaster. His loose skin was pale and tissue-thin, with a web of capillaries and fascia beneath the translucent surface, as if this was all he was, a hologram of viscera hobbling inexorably toward the junk heap.

Webb reached into the truck and pulled out a briny slab of skipjack wrapped in plastic.

"Can't fish salmon, can't use hatch boxes. Governor's gonna bankrupt the state," said George.

Webb brought the fish into the store and placed them on a stainless steel table. He removed two bags of ice from the stockroom freezer, then dropped them into a bus tray and carried them out to the store. Tearing them open, he emptied them into the display case. He did this three times before standing in front of the large pile of ice. George watched him through the glass. Webb reached in and smoothed the ice with his hands. He worked fast, grabbing large frozen chunks he snapped them, breaking them into small pieces. Within seconds his skin burned as the freeze radiated to the bone.

George insisted that Webb spread the ice without gloves. Gloves carried germs, he said, contaminated the fish, so Webb kept his head low and spread the ice while George watched. His hands ached but he did nothing, didn't ball them into fists or fan the fingers to get the circulation going. He was not going to let George Plotki see him suffer.

It took less than a minute before he lost all sensation, less than a minute before his hands were useless clubs. George stood on the other side of the glass, railing against the newest fishing regulation, but Webb couldn't hear a word. All he could hear was the sound of the ocean in his ears, the waves crashing against the beach like they did when he was a boy casting his rod into the water from the slick, black rock that jutted into the surf. It had been disturbing at first, this loss of sensation, but in recent months he had begun to imagine that he was handless, incapable of committing the crime for which he had been convicted, and he found that he could quiet, at least for a moment, its memory. It was in these brief moments, before walking to the stockroom to run warm water over his hands, that Webb Cooley clung to the dim illusion that he was not a man who had murdered his wife.

5

He was arranging tins of cough mints on the counter when she entered, holding a wet newspaper over her head. She pulled a tangle of hair from her face. He glanced back to see George watching him. George pulled open the top drawer of his desk and cracked open a fresh pack of American Spirits.

Alice dropped a granola bar on the counter. He rang her up.

"You don't happen to know if there's a pawn shop around here?"

She had blonde hair and a sprinkling of freckles across her nose.

"You could try Mitzi up the street at Secondhand Treasures."

He watched her walk to the door. He inhaled, trying to catch her scent. He followed her with his eyes, her round hips swinging as she walked to the door.

And then she was gone.

George watched Webb from the stockroom, smiling, a cigarette dangling from his lips.

*   *   *

Alice climbed the sidewalk past a two-story stone apartment building and pushed open the front door of the U.S. Post Office and Secondhand Treasures. The windows were darkened with silver foil. She walked through a maze of furniture and knick-knacks. A cat stretched on top of a china hutch. As her eyes adjusted she saw cats everywhere. "Hello? Somebody here?"

"Where'dya park?" growled a voice from the back.

"At the hotel."

"That's good, cause they're ticketing now. Anything to make a buck." The only light came from a couple of candles near the back of the room. The red glow from a cigarette illuminated the outline of a human form. "Ya staying there?"

"Just for last night," said Alice.

"Say hi to my man Milo for me."

Alice approached the figure wearing a royal blue U.S. Postal Service uniform over a shapeless frame.

"Is Milo the guy at the desk?"

"Yeah."

"Are you Mitzi?"

"That's right. Now let me guess. You're looking for an umbrella."

Alice shook her head. "Do you take trade-ins?"

"What ya peddlin'?" Mitzi had the creviced face of a heavy smoker, and when she spoke, Alice noticed a gap where an incisor used to be. A sign on the register read: *Please take all donations around to back of store.*

Alice tugged off her wedding ring and placed it on the counter. Mitzi studied it, then puckered her lips and breathed a stream of smoke out the side of her mouth.

"Sure it's over?"

Alice nodded.

Mitzi picked a fleck of tobacco off her tongue. "What do you want for it?"

"I guess I'd take a thousand. It cost way more than that."

Mitzi slid the ring back across the counter.

"How much were *you* thinking?"

Mitzi squinted. "Seventy-five."

"That's over two carats," said Alice.

Mitzi took a puff and returned to her magazine. "Joyce is looking for help. Try the craft store a block over."

"I'm not looking for work. I just want to get out of here."

"When you go outside, make a right, otherwise you'll have to walk up the hill again."

Alice stared at the ring. She shoved it into her purse.

6

She stood at the curb. The sky was flat. At the bottom of the hill a row of ducks paddled after their mother. She went down her checklist of options—then cursed. What am I doing here?

She wondered what she would say to him. She didn't want his money. She just wanted enough to get to Seattle.

So, why was she shaking?

Because it would be so easy to go back to him.

Before she married him, she spoke to his previous ex-wife, Kendra, a miniature bombshell, funny and smart with a dirty mouth. She was tougher than Alice, and told her everything she needed to know. Yes, she said, Chick is a genius, and fascinating, and impulsive, but he will not adapt to you ahhhht aaaall. It's lonely, she told her. And Alice listened, but she didn't understand.

One night, after playing a show at New York City's Beacon Theater, Chick asked her to marry him. He was high from the show, and she was high from being his girlfriend. Plus, he was pretty decent looking, tallish, shaggy, and musician fit—

meaning skinny, but with no muscle tone, except in his fingers.

She told her friends that she was engaged to Chick Wolfson and they were suitably impressed. She discovered ways to bring it up in conversation with strangers. She'd be buying shoes, and would laugh, and then apologize for laughing by telling the salesperson, "Sorry, that's my fiancé on the radio," and then she would crack a joke, "I'm still adjusting to this"— and they would be charmed and amazed. Or she would be in line at the DMV and would ask the girl in front of her, "Are you a musician? Oh, what do you play? Oh, my husband plays the piano." Until it emerged quite naturally that she was Chick Wolfson's main squeeze, and she would gauge what that meant to the girl. She was collecting data, trying to cull from this random sample of strangers how she should feel about her future husband.

And then she stopped painting.

Just stopped.

He looked at one of her paintings, and asked, "Is that supposed to be a frog?"

That was it. That was all he said. But she replayed it endlessly in her head. "Is that *supposed* to be a frog?" What did he mean? Did he hate it? Was her art terrible? Was she kidding herself? He just blinked and walked away—and she couldn't breathe for weeks. She shoved it down, pushed, kept pushing until she couldn't feel it anymore. But there was a part of her that hated him. Hated. But she couldn't admit it because that would spoil it for the part that would do anything to be in his presence.

He even asked her once, "How come you never paint anymore?" She stared at him in shock until the moment passed.

He was a brutal critic, contemptuous of his rock star friends. He didn't hand out compliments. He won their approval through humor. He teasingly complimented their *success*, which was his backhanded way of dismissing their work while reminding them that he was the one who had not sold out.

She couldn't paint around him. It was easier to stop, easier to do nothing. Kendra warned her, don't lose yourself, he will swallow you whole, there's only room for one genius in the household.

Chick answered the phone. He made a noise, like a chuckle. "So, you finally escaped me, huh?"

When she was with him, everything she said sounded dumb. She swallowed. "Yup."

"Well . . . that puts a crimp in my week."

"Please don't be glib," she said.

"Sure," he said. "And would you mind not making unilateral decisions on our marriage based on some romantic notion you read about in a fantasy book when you were seven?"

"I want to talk."

"Fine. Come home. Let's talk."

"I don't know if I want to do that," she said. "It doesn't feel like a home." She watched the ducks fighting their way across the river. "Are you there?"

"Yeah, I was just writing that down. I'm keeping a book of clichés."

"Fuck you."

"I'm not doing this on a phone, Alice. Come back and we'll talk."

"But we won't. We won't talk."

"All right," he sighed. "Talk."

She didn't know what to say. All she could think about was his comment about the frog. "Why did you say 'Is that supposed to be a frog?' when you looked at my painting?"

"I've never seen you paint."

"Right before we got married, I showed you one of my paintings and you asked me if it was supposed to be a frog."

"Before we got married?"

"Yes."

"And what's your point?"

"You didn't like it, did you? You were criticizing it."

"Asking if it was a frog was criticizing it?"

"That's not my point. I just mean, you never said you liked it."

"So what?"

"You never encouraged me."

"There was nothing to encourage," he said. "You never did anything."

"You didn't want me to!"

"Let me get this straight. You're leaving me because thirteen years ago I asked you if you'd painted a frog?"

"You're doing it again. You do this all the time. You twist everything. It threatens you that other people might create something interesting too."

"Hello Freud? Can you help me out?"

"Don't make fun of me."

"What happened to you while I was gone?"

"Do you love me?"

"What?"

"When you love somebody you encourage them."

"If you were a real artist, you wouldn't be looking to me for encouragement."

Alice was silent. She could feel it happening, the gradual imploding, like her lungs were folding in on themselves, like talking required too much air. "I didn't want to lose you," she said. "I felt like I didn't have a choice. You can deny it, but you didn't want me painting."

"Wrong," he said.

"You wanted me available to you. It was a nice life, Chick, but it's not for me."

He chuckled. "You sound like all the others."

"I probably am."

"Are all women hardwired to blame their husbands for their failed dreams?"

"Is that what you think I'm doing?"

"No. It *is* what you're doing."

"I wish you could have shown a little interest in me."

"Okay," he said. "Are you done?"

"Sure. I'm done."

"So, it sounds like you've made up your mind."

She could feel herself being pulled into his vortex. It was inexplicable. She wanted to tell him, no, she had not made up her mind. She wanted him to change her mind.

"I wish we could talk," she said. "I wish we could communicate."

She heard the sizzle of a joint being lit.

"You mean, like humans do?"

"Nothing changes, Chick. I don't know who you are, and you don't seem at all curious about me."

"No. I just don't relate to the neurotic impulse to blow up a long-term marriage over a misperceived slight that happened over thirteen years ago. Did it occur to you to bring that up before we got married? Could you please put my wife on the phone, the one who is rational, at least most of the time?"

"I'm right here."

He sucked on the joint. "I'm not going to control you. You want to leave, leave."

No, she wanted to scream. If he fought for her, she would return to him in a second. "I just want you to hear me," she said.

"Uh huh," he said, but he was already high.

She fought for the words. "Really?" she said. Thirteen years? That's all you have to say? If I'm going to leave, leave? That's not controlling me, Chick. That's indifference."

"I'm not the one who left."

"Actually, yes you are," she said.

And then there was silence, like they were waiting for the other one to speak. She wondered if it was a power struggle, or if it was just that neither of them cared enough to repair things.

"You do realize this whimsical decision you're making is permanent," he said.

Was this a game to him, she wondered, or was he really this cold?

She hung up.

She walked down the hill. A light rain fell. Droplets landed on her cheeks but she couldn't feel them.

Alice went into the lobby of the Frontier and dialed her mother.

7

"Honey, what is it?" said Trish. "I called you this morning. Did you get my message?"

"No."

"Is Chick back? I think you said he was getting back yesterday."

"He's back."

"Oh, good. You must have missed him."

"Mom, listen. I'm driving up to surprise you."

"What? Where are you?"

"Well, it was supposed to be a surprise. I'm in Oregon, and . . ."

"Are you joking with me?"

"I'm not joking."

"Oh, I can't wait to see you."

"There's just a little problem. I don't have any money."

"Don't you have a card? Can you get some from Chick?"

"I don't want to bother him with it." She had never lied to her mother before. Not outright. But this was different. She was asking for money under false pretenses, and it made her feel like shit.

"Sweetheart, I'm sure Chick isn't going to mind giving you a few dollars to come see us."

"Mom, I just . . . don't want to ask him."

"Why? Are you okay? Did something happen?"

This was not how she planned it.

"I'm fine. I just . . ."

"Then why can't you get some money from him? He must have made some money on his trip."

"It was a tour, Mom, not a trip. And he did. I can probably ask him. Okay, fine, I'll ask him."

"Alice, talk to me. Tell me what's going on."

Alice started to cry. "I just haven't been happy for a long time. I'm taking a break from him."

"What happened?"

"Nothing! Nothing happened. I just . . . you're not going to understand. I already know you're not going to understand."

"Tell me."

"I'm just not happy. I'm not."

"But something must have happened."

"No. That's the thing. I can't explain it. I don't know if I've ever been happy. I don't know if I ever really loved him."

Trish laughed. "I'm sorry, honey. I went through the same thing with your father."

"Mom, I'm not joking."

"No, I know you're not."

"He cut off my cards. I don't have any money."

"Why did he do that?"

"Because I said I wanted to take a break."

"You said that? Oh, you don't say that."

Alice felt a trickle of sweat run down her back.

"Things change in a marriage. It's not the same as it was in the beginning."

"That's not what I'm talking about. I think I married him for the wrong reasons. I keep waiting for something to change to make it tolerable. I feel like I made a horrible mistake, and I keep waiting for him to change, and I just don't want to leave, but I can't stay any longer. And I don't want you to talk me out of this."

"I'm not going to talk you out of it, but this is going to pass, I promise."

"You're already doing it. It's never passing. I've always felt like this."

"You can't walk out. It's not good for a marriage. Let me send you the money. Where are you?"

"I'm in Oregon."

"I'll give you my credit card number. You can buy what you need and come up here and stay with us as long as you want."

"No. I can't."

"Why not?"

"Because I know you. You're going to talk me into going back to him."

There was a pause.

She said, "We won't do that."

The ducks had paddled to the other side of the river. They hopped out of the water and shook their tails.

"Sweetheart, you have to go back to him. I mean, let's be serious."

Alice hung up.

8

She walked down Main Street. Her phone buzzed. It was her mother calling back. She hit IGNORE and shut it off. At the bottom of the hill she turned the corner at the bank. The next block was Second Street. She climbed back up the hill, and as she neared the top she saw a hand-painted sign that read *Notions and Appliances* above a small storefront. In the window a refrigerator and stove stood next to a stack of quilts and a bushel basket filled with brightly colored rolls of yarn.

Alice turned the door handle and entered. A tall woman in a plum tracksuit and heavy make-up greeted her. "Look at you, you skinny thing," she said. "How can I help you?"

"I heard you might be looking for some help?"

"Oh yeah? Says who?"

"Mitzi, from the post office."

Alice glanced around the store. One wall was lined with refrigerators, stoves, washers and dryers, while the rest of the store contained small craft booths displaying everything from handmade cushions and welcome mats to soy candles and cat toys. In the corner, a woman was crouched on her hands and knees scrubbing the inside of an oven.

"Well, she's not wrong," said Joyce. "Who are you?"

Alice stiffened. Maybe it was from all the years of living with Chick, but she suddenly felt stuck answering such a broad question, as if she was sure to get it wrong. "Um . . ."

"I mean, what's your name? Where'dya come from? How'dya hear about me?"

"Oh, I'm Alice."

"Nice to meet you. I'm Joyce."

"I'm from San Francisco. I just moved here," she lied.

"Are you married? Single?"

"Actually," Alice sighed, "I just separated from my husband."

"Really?" Joyce looked her up and down. "So, what on earth brings you here?" She glanced at the woman scrubbing the oven in the corner. "Trudy, she musta heard about my store?" And then she laughed, a machine-gun rat-a-tat-tat. Trudy pushed her hair from her eyes and stared at Alice.

"Hi there," said Alice, but Trudy just gazed at her, slack-jawed.

"I'm looking for a job," Alice said to Joyce.

"I know. I got that part. I'll be honest, I usually go on referral," said Joyce. "Do you have retail experience?"

"I used to work at an art gallery."

"We're sorta different than an art gallery, like maybe the opposite. I don't want you being snobby and ignoring people," she said. And then she laughed again. Rat-a-tat- tat. "This ain't the big city where we intimidate folks into buying a tea cozy. I need friendly."

"I can be friendly."

"I'm teasing," said Joyce. "Heck, you're a sensitive one. Hey

Trudy! Come here for a minute."

Trudy pulled her head out of the oven and hovered over to them with her hands pressed to her thighs.

"This is Alice. Does she look friendly to you?"

Trudy lifted her frail shoulders. "I guess."

"Thank you," said Alice.

"Trudy comes in three times a week, but I just use her to clean," said Joyce. "I need someone a little more put together to work with the ladies."

Alice blinked. She looked at Trudy who stood motionless, awaiting further instructions.

"Thanks, Trudy," said Joyce, waving her away.

Trudy returned to the oven and shoved her head back inside.

"I'll tell you what I'm gonna do. I'm gonna try you out for a week and let's see how it goes. Does that sound okay to you?"

Alice nodded.

"Fabulous," said Joyce. "We pay nine-ten an hour with a seventy-five cent raise after six months. I can give you twenty percent off any merchandise in the store. Where are you living?"

"The Frontier."

Joyce winced. "Oh, good grief. You can't stay there."

"I know. It's brutal."

Joyce squealed. She threw an arm around her. "Oh, I think we're gonna get along."

She led Alice to the back where she filled a bucket, and then she led her to the refrigerator, patted her shoulder and toddled away. Alice fell to her knees next to Trudy. She opened the fridge door and her stomach flew up at the stench.

"Fridges are the grossest," said Trudy.

"They better be."

Later that morning Joyce bent down and whispered, "I know someone you should meet."

"I'm not looking to meet anyone."

"His name's Lester," said Joyce. "He's an attorney."

"He has a hot tub," said Trudy.

9

At lunchtime, Alice asked Joyce where she could get a cheap bite to eat. Joyce directed her to Corky's, a ramshackle diner with yellow paint peeling off its wooden siding. Inside, thick redwood tables lined the perimeter of the room, with deep booths in the two back corners. The walls were made of plywood. A bluegrass station played in the background. She watched a young man with a shaved head and a tattoo on the back of his neck spread mayonnaise on her turkey sandwich in the kitchen. The restaurant was half full. She felt raw from her conversation with Chick and was glad to be alone after spending the morning pretending everything was okay. She wanted to hurt Chick, and was now furious with herself for signing a prenuptial agreement. She'd never told her parents about it, though her mother asked her once, "Honey, it's none of my business, but you didn't sign any kind of a prenup, did you?"

"What?!"

"Never mind."

"God, Mom."

And that was it. She never denied it. She just acted suitably horrified, and it was never discussed again.

A man in a navy trench coat and cowboy boots entered the diner. He was good-looking in a TV commercial kind of way. With his strong chin and doughy cheeks he had the kind of face that could sell a jeep. He had large white teeth and chewed on a hunk of gum with bovine glee. His eyes shot around the restaurant and he waved to a whippet-thin man in a knit cap sitting in the booth at the back. "I'll be right there, Ned." There was a motion to him, like his motor was revved, like he had pressing matters to attend to, and he dressed differently than everyone else, like he was the only man in town with a desk job. Under his coat he wore a burgundy V-neck sweater over a white dress shirt. Chick would have called him a *sweater man*. Chick had a theory that there were two kinds of men in the world, sweater men and jacket men, and though he conceded to some overlap, if you wore a sweater you were likely a person whose occupation was secured through years of regurgitating information. Whether a waiter or an accountant, to be the best meant that you excelled at learning a system. Sweater men were cogs. Sweater men worked well with rules, but never with ideas. There were other kinds of sweater men; although salesmen were often required to wear jackets for work, at heart they were sweater men too because according to Chick their goal in life was to perfect a system. His theory was based on the notion that all things being equal, if you had to choose between a sweater and a jacket, your choice said everything about who you were on the most fundamental level, from risk-tolerance to political affiliation to sexual appetite to spiritual evolution. He went on for weeks, elaborating on his theory, and even wrote a song about it. "Sweater Man" became the song he chose to kick off his *Care*

Less CD. He explained to Alice that being a sweater man was really about being soft, about maintaining the status quo, about sleepwalking through life, that sweaters were cocoons meant to metaphorically wrap you in denial. Alice nodded thoughtfully, while wondering if it was a coincidence that her husband's theory was hatched over breakfast following a barbecue at a friend's house where he overdressed in a jacket on a chilly night that saw the majority of the men wearing sweaters.

The man in the trench coat looked at Alice and smiled. It was a practiced smile, but a good one. His eyes crinkled in the corners. "I'm sorry," he said. "You look familiar." His voice was pleasant, like a purr. "Have we met?"

She shook her head. "I don't think so."

"You're not from around here?"

"No."

"Do you mind if I sit down?" he asked after sitting down. "Phyllis," he said to the waitress. "Could I get a cup of coffee?"

"Sure thing, Les."

"I'm Lester," he said to Alice, holding out his hand.

She shook it. "Alice."

"So, are you just passing through?"

"No," she lied. "I just moved here."

"Is that your Volvo across the street?"

"You're very observant."

"It's a small town. We don't get a lot of visitors," he said. "What part of California are you from?"

"San Francisco."

"I figured," he said. "You got that look."

"That look?"

"Like you've read a book."

She noticed his leg bouncing up and down nervously under the counter.

"What brings you up this way?"

She shrugged. "The friendly people."

He grinned. "Are you kidding me?"

"Only a little," she said.

He laughed. "Listen, I got a client over there that I have to speak to, but would you be . . ."

"Are you a lawyer?"

"Yeah, how'd you know?"

"Just a wild guess. So, what'd he do?"

Lester glanced at Ned Feeney sitting in the corner pouring packets of sugar into his coffee. With his gaunt, scarred face and knit cap he looked a full two decades older than his twenty-five years. "Ned shot a Mexican in the knuckle over a patch of mushrooms."

"He looks like a serial killer."

"I know. And apparently I'm related to him in some tangential way."

"Scary," she said.

"Definitely not something to brag about. Listen, I don't want to be too forward, but would you like to get dinner with me tonight?"

"Well gosh," she said, "I'm flattered, Lester, but I'm actually married, so . . ."

"Yeah, but aren't you sep—" he began, and then stopped. "So, where's your husband?"

Suddenly Alice understood what was happening. "He's back in San Francisco," she said. "But you already knew that."

"I did?" he said.

She nodded. "Joyce called and told you that I was here, didn't she?"

"Oh boy." He blushed. "I'm busted."

"Yeah, you are," she said. "What are you, the local eligible bachelor that everyone's trying to marry off?"

"Pretty much."

"I hear you have a hot tub."

"Oh geez, you were talking to Trudy. I let the ladies use my house for a craft sale over the summer. Now every time I see her she wants to talk about my hot tub."

"Well, I appreciate the offer, but I'm just not looking to meet anyone right now."

"No problem, I got it," he said.

Ned stood up at the back of the restaurant. "Hey, Les, are we gonna get this going or not?" he asked.

"Ned, relax. I'll be right there," said Lester. He turned back to Alice. "He's a rude little bastard. Anyway, I better get, but listen, if you need anything, just let me know." He opened his wallet. "Here's my card."

"Thank you," she said.

He picked up his coffee and walked back to meet his client. "Ned!" He raised his hand and high-fived him. "You gotta learn some manners, kiddo," he said.

10

Alice returned to the store to find a group of women sitting in the middle of the room working on various craft projects for their booths. Joyce gave Alice a basket of buttons to separate by color and size.

"So you're living here now?" asked a large woman with a patrician face who painted cat whiskers and ears onto smooth little stones.

"Yes. I just moved here yesterday," said Alice.

A woman in black tights and pink sneakers sat on the floor making a necklace out of shells. "Joyce says you left your old man. Was he unfaithful?"

"If he was, he's a fool," said a woman who bent hanger wires into shapes that vaguely resembled monkeys. "Look at that figure!"

"Don't make a difference to some men."

"Is she right?" asked the woman in the pink sneakers.

Alice shook her head. "No," she whispered.

"I can't imagine leaving Dan," said the woman painting cat

whiskers. "Even if he cheated, I couldn't just walk out."

"I'm guessing she doesn't have children. Do you have children, Ally?"

"It's Alice," she said. "No. I don't."

"Didn't want 'em, or . . . ?"

Alice could feel herself falling away. "I don't know," she said. She thought back a year ago, to the time Chick casually mentioned to their friends that he had recently gotten a vasectomy while on the road.

Afterwards, she asked him, "Why didn't you tell me?"

"What difference does it make?" he said. "We're never having kids."

It was true. From the beginning he told her that he never wanted kids, and she agreed. "That's not the point," she said. "You should have told me."

"It never came up," he said.

"Because you never brought it up."

"I did it on the road so it wouldn't interfere with our sex life."

"Then why didn't you get one twelve years ago?"

"Never got around to it," he said. "Why are you so upset?"

"Because you don't trust me," she said. "I could have gotten pregnant a million times, but I didn't."

She had begun talking about wanting to have a baby, and he never said anything. He never fought with her. He just called a doctor and had a procedure.

"You just do whatever you want," she said.

His eyes twinkled.

"For the past six months I've been talking about having a baby and you've been keeping this secret from me! I feel like an idiot. You could have said something. You're a vampire. Don't you have any emotions?!"

"None that you can relate to."

She wept, screamed, told him she wanted to die. She moved into a hotel for a week, and then moved back and never spoke about it again. They had sex, more frequently than before, but now it was different. She used to climax by imagining that she was making love to Chick Wolfson, but now it was only possible when she imagined that he was someone, anyone, else. She had spent her life seeking a relationship that could offer her precisely this heart-pounding experience only to realize that what she thought was sexual attraction was actually fear. Being married to a man that made her heart race led to anxiety and exhaustion. Lately she began to wonder what it would be like to share her life with someone who made her heart slow down.

Alice couldn't distinguish the colors of the buttons. She dropped them randomly into boxes and watched them all swim together.

"Is she crying?"

"I need to use the restroom," said Alice.

"It's okay, dear," said Joyce.

"What's the matter?" said the woman bending wire into monkeys. "What did we say?"

Joyce squeezed Alice's shoulder and guided her to her feet. She brought her to the back room, but Alice could still hear the women talking about her from the other side of the wall.

11

After work, Alice went back to the Frontier. She approached Milo sitting at the front desk. From the way he sat, leaned back in his chair, it looked to Alice like he was sleeping.

"Excuse me," she said. "You're Milo, right?"

He nodded.

"I don't get paid till Friday. I'm working up the street and I was wondering if I could pay you on Friday . . ."

"Gimme your watch," he said.

She glanced at her antique watch, the one her mother gave her when she graduated from high school.

"This is worth a lot more than a week's rent."

"You'll get it back when you pay your rent," he said.

She pulled it off her wrist and placed it on the counter.

12

Mrs. Packer studied Webb suspiciously as she entered the store. She was an old widow, frail and thin. Taking a box of Stillman cinnamon cookies from the shelf, she dropped it into her basket. "Good morning, Mr. Plotki."

George nodded from his desk in the stock room. "How are you today, Mrs. Packer?"

"The potholes are full of water. I can't tell when it's road and when it's hole." She walked up the aisle toward the cash register.

George dropped his newspaper on the desk and pulled himself to his feet. Webb stepped backwards from the counter while George limped up the aisle to the register. Mrs. Packer kept her eyes on the floor as George pushed past Webb and took the bag of cookies from the old lady.

"Did you hear about Ned Feeney?" she said. "I don't know what those Mexicans are thinking coming around here. I'm sure they're not legal."

"Course they're not," said George, handing the cookies to Webb, who placed them in a bag.

It was mushroom season and the chanterelles that grew in the woods along the coast attracted immigrant entrepreneurs. Each fall, vanloads of Mexicans drove north and battled the locals for the lucrative crop. The previous week, Ned challenged a couple of Mexicans over poaching on his claim. He pulled a gun, and when the Mexican bent to pick another mushroom, Ned blew off his knuckle.

"I don't approve of what Ned did, but they got no business being here," said Mrs. Packer. "He's just gonna stir 'em up." She wrote a check for the cookies.

"Or send 'em home."

"They're not coming in here, are they?"

"They buy all my beans," said George. Webb handed the bag to the old man, who handed it to Mrs. Packer.

"*You* have a nice day, Mr. Plotki."

"You too," he said as she walked to the door. "Miserable bitch," he muttered, and shuffled back to the stock room.

*   *   *

Alice walked into the general store and approached Webb at the counter. "Excuse me. Do you know where I can find someone to fix the lock on my door?"

"There's a hardware store up the street."

"I'm almost flat out of money."

George walked up the aisle. "Frontier won't fix it?"

"Not till Monday."

George stared at her legs and sniffed. "Cooley, you could help her."

Webb nodded.

"We got a tool box in back. Wait till six, he'll do it for you."

"Thank you," said Alice.

*   *   *

Alice stood at the window watching Webb through the reflection in the glass. His shirtsleeves were rolled up revealing thick veins that snaked along his forearms. A blue prison tattoo on the inside of his arm read: karen. There was a power through his trunk that made her think of a wolf.

He held up a piece of twisted metal that blocked the shaft. "Here's your culprit."

A shadow crossed behind him.

"Ain't you a neighbor," said Percy, his head bobbed lazily. "Fixing her lock?" he said to Alice, but the way he said it, he meant something else. "You don't talk to me no more," he said to Webb, like it was a threat.

Webb squeezed the screwdriver. The blood drained from his knuckles. "How you doing, Percy?"

"Like you care," said Percy.

The two men looked at each other. Alice wondered if something was about to happen, then Percy just smirked and disappeared down the hall.

Alice wanted to say something, lighten the mood, but when she looked at Webb's face, it was pale. His eyes were hard, and she changed her mind.

He stood with the piece of twisted metal in his hand. "Well. You have a good night."

"You too," she said.

He walked down the hall.

"What's your name?" she asked.

He turned. "I'm Webb."

"I'm Alice."

He nodded. "Okay," he said. "You'll sleep better with that door locked."

"Thank you."

He hoisted his toolbox, almost like he was trying to salute. He felt foolish, like he was saying, if you ever need help, I'm always here. "Good night," he said.

"Good night, Webb."

She went into her room and locked the door. She held onto the knob. It was still warm. She repeated his name. He had a quiet masculine strength; when he walked, his feet landed solidly. Chick was wiry, and usually high, and always looked like he was about to tip over. Webb's hands were wide and thick, made for labor, while Chick's were long and elegant. Even the way each of them spoke, the way they formed their thoughts was opposite. Webb was plain spoken, while Chick measured his words for effect. He used language for sport. Her conversations with him left her depleted. He was never straight with her. There was always a subtext, an agenda she could never follow.

Why am I comparing them? she wondered. I'm still married, she told herself—at least, technically. Besides, she wasn't leaving Chick to replace him. She wanted to be alone, to reconnect to herself, to trace the etiology of this thirteen year misstep. What she did not want was another man. In fact, she rarely thought about other men, at least, not in that way. When she fantasized, it was usually some sweeping scenario that involved passionate lovemaking with a faceless feudal lord in a castle beneath high thread-count sheets while being fanned by a team of rippled-muscled eunuchs. She did not fantasize about being unfaithful, at least, not with anyone living, although she once imagined a threesome with Clinton and Bush, but realized later it was not a sex dream but a bipartisan attempt to repair her parents' lack of intimacy.

For several years into her marriage, Chick *was* her fantasy, her escape, and it was her attempts to coax him from the subterranean corridors of her fevered dreams into a workable marriage that led her to where she was now.

She went to the window and watched Webb walk up the street. He kept his head low. She wondered if he was shielding it from the rain, or from something else. She watched until he fell out of view, and then she took her clothes off and got ready for bed.

*   *   *

Webb climbed the sidewalk. The rain fell hard. He kept his eyes on the water rolling down the pavement in waves of braided semi-circles. From across the street he heard the rumble of men's voices inside the Pastime Tavern. He reached his building and pushed open the door, then climbed the stairs to his apartment.

He placed the toolbox on the floor of his room and turned on the heater. It clicked and coughed before a fine geyser of steam spewed from a crack in the knob. He kept the room hot, like it had been in prison. He stripped to his underwear and did pushups, elbows tight at his ribs, muscles straining until his back was slick with sweat. He fell to the floor, breathing heavily, remembering how it felt when she said his name.

13

At midnight, Alice heard footsteps down the hall, and then the door next to hers opened and shut. A moment later the sound of Bob Dylan's nasal reprimand blasted through the wall. She covered her head with a pillow, but it made no difference. She went into the hall and knocked on the door.

"Percy, get lost."

"It's not Percy."

The music stopped. Alice heard rustling inside. The door cracked open and two huge dark eyes stared back at her. She was a head taller than Alice, with a thick neck and massive shoulders. Her lips were full on one side then tapered to almost nothing. A pair of plush breasts fell rudely over her belly. She wore a flannel shirt and a pair of men's boxers and spoke in a raw husky voice. "What do you want?"

"Would you mind keeping your music down?"

She scanned Alice's figure, then slammed the door. A moment passed before the music began again.

Alice pounded on the door. "Hey!" Percy peeked out.

Alice glared at him and he disappeared back inside.

The door flew open. "I don't turn my music down for nobody, you skinny bitch."

"Just don't slam the door in my face."

"This is my turf, you little scab," she looked over her shoulder. "Percy, get back in your room or I'll cut that thing off!"

With his right shoulder working busily, Percy grimaced through a mouth of broken teeth.

"Jesus," said Alice.

"Like you never seen that before," said the woman. "Percy, I said close it!"

"Just keep your music down." Alice walked back to her room.

"You ain't Ricky's favorite for long," said the woman. "You wait and see."

"Who the hell is Ricky?"

"Oh puh-leeze. They don't like your type here anyhow. This is lumber country." She squeezed her breasts. "They want tits and ass, not your scrawny shit."

Alice closed her door.

"Tits and ass!" the woman shouted.

Alice climbed back into bed, but the music was louder now. The room shook as the woman pounded the wall with the end of a stick. She threw off the blanket and went back into the hallway.

"Hey!" Alice banged on the door. "I'm not a stripper." The music went silent. "I said I'm not a goddamn stripper!"

"Ha!"

Alice was about to re-enter her room when the woman peeked out wrapped in a thin army blanket, clutching the corners at her neck.

"Nor am I," she said, batting her lashes. "I entertain in

the traditional burlesque genre of my fore-sisters." She had hurriedly applied rouge to her cheeks without blending it in. She looked insane.

"I just want some sleep," said Alice.

Percy peeked out from behind his door. The woman's face twisted. "Percy, go to hell! We're trying to have a civilized conversation here."

"Suck me," he said. His door swung open. He was naked. Coarse tufts of black hair covered his body like a blanket of houseflies.

"I wouldn't suck you for diamonds. Now get lost or I'll get Milo."

"I ain't scared of Milo," he said. He slammed his door.

"You are too!" She turned to Alice. "He is too. He's like a frightened little mouse." She extended her hand. "Anyway, I'm Ruth. Like in the Bible." Alice introduced herself. Ruth tilted her head toward her room. "Would you care to partake in some sacramental hemp?"

"I can't," said Alice. "I have to get up early."

Ruth rolled her eyes. "Suit yourself."

"But it was nice to meet you."

"It always is."

*   *   *

Alice lay in bed staring at the light coming through the curtains. The mattress spring dug into her side. She wriggled on the bed, trying to arrange her body to avoid it. The room was dusty. Everything was damp; the sheets, the curtains, the carpet, it all smelled like mold. She tried to think about anything other than where she was. Her mind flashed on Webb. She replayed the moment when Percy walked past him and said, "You don't talk to me no more." She wondered what it meant. Had they been friends? She turned on her side and felt the spring follow her. She remembered her bed back in San Francisco, a king-sized custom-built mattress Chick ordered from a company in Maine. It was like sleeping on a cloud.

What was Chick doing right now?

Was he out with friends, spinning the tale of how she bolted minutes before he returned from tour? Had he turned her into a joke yet, like he did with his ex-wives? What did his friends think of her now? Were they surprised? After thirteen years of marriage, of losing herself in his world, there was no one she felt close enough to confide in. She had tried to call Kendra, his previous ex, but it was a decade since they last spoke, and her phone number was disconnected. She wasn't sure how it happened, how all of her friends fell away. No. That was a lie. She knew exactly how it happened; she was in San Francisco for two years, studying at the Art Institute of S.F., where she developed friendships with other girls and was even dating another boy, but when she met Chick, she cleared the decks. In retrospect, she panicked. She made a conscious decision to become someone else, this vaunted version of herself, sophisticated, wise beyond her years, an old soul. She was twenty-three and Chick was forty-two, so giggling was out. She didn't want to lose him, so she dumped her friends and adopted his. And it worked. She got what she wanted.

She played the role of devoted wife for so long that it was too embarrassing to admit, even to herself, that it was false. The realization crept up on her slowly, and it was difficult to reconcile her growing ambivalence toward Chick with the plushness of their life together. They lived in a contemporary three-bedroom penthouse co-op on Hill Street with spectacular 180-degree views and every amenity. When she needed dry-cleaning done, she called the concierge. Gourmet meals were delivered in a cooler on ice three times a week. There was a spa on the second floor where she swam each morning and got a massage weekly. When they traveled, they stayed at The Four Seasons or The Ritz Carlton, and always flew first class. They were regulars at Chez Panisse. People whispered when she walked into a room with Chick. She was, by proximity, always the focus of attention, and she liked it, it gave her a charge, a persistent, low-grade buzz. He was high on grass, and she was high on being Mrs. Chick Wolfson.

She detested the part of herself that enjoyed the attention because it challenged the part that insisted she married him for his integrity and musical genius, which was true, except there was no love, not really, not the kind that bloomed—there was heat, and in the beginning she believed that was enough, but when it faded their love did not ripen into long breakfast chats and leisurely hikes through Muir Woods. The veneer of their perfect union began to wear almost immediately until it became inescapable to her that she chose to marry him not for reasons of chemistry or even a practical desire to build a family, since he already had an adult son from his first marriage and made it clear he did not want to make any more, but, quite simply, because he was famous. She shuddered when she realized that he could have been anyone, that their marriage was, for each of them, though in entirely different ways, a flight from reality. This revelation was so intolerable to her that she buried it. To leave him would make it true, and so she stayed to protect all of the ideas she had about herself. After all, she was from Seattle, from good, humble stock. Her parents valued their privacy, went out of their way to not draw attention. Yes, their home verged on palatial, but it was nestled behind a tall hedge. Her father repeatedly declined interviews after winning large settlements for his clients. He understood, and inculcated into his wife and daughter that the secret to life was hard work and service to others, and that it was fine to enjoy the fruit of one's labor, but that the greatest sin was to be seen as anything more than ordinary. Therefore Alice was horrified to realize that the biggest decision in her life was motivated by a whorish bid to be special.

But it was.

She couldn't shut her mind off. How would she make it till morning? She threw off the covers and went into the hall. She stood in front of Ruth's door and hesitated for a moment before knocking.

14

"Grab a seat," said Ruth. Alice scanned the room before settling on the edge of the bed. The room was stark, lit by a single bulb. Clothes were strewn on the floor and a peeling cardboard trunk sat open under the window.

Ruth struck a match against the wall and lit a joint. "I've been getting it from the same guy for years." She inhaled deeply. "This vet buys it by the vanload in Humboldt County, drives it up to Portland . . ." She gasped, blasting out a plume of smoke. "He's all right, got a bit of a foot fetish. He cradles my feet for an hour in exchange for an ounce of the best dope on the west coast." She handed the joint to Alice. "Sweetheart, I know what you're wondering," she said, waving a meaty hand. "But if you're gonna hang with Ruthie you gotta understand one thing: I'm a renaissance gal. I've been respectable and I've been disrespectable. I spent a year as the mayor of Vegas' executive secretary, then he got mixed up in some scandal and I moved on. Yes, my current employ requires I be primarily de-robed, but that's just the tip of this iceberg."

Alice took a puff. "So you thought I was a . . . dancer?"

Ruth narrowed her eyes. "Ricky keeps threatening to can my butt if I don't drop some weight. Says one day I'll come to town and there'll be another girl in my place." She took the joint from Alice. "He's a douchebag. Least his old man paid what he said he would."

"He sounds like one."

"He said I got a face like a slab of bacon."

"You have beautiful eyes."

"Can it, Janet. I know what I got. I appeal to the discerning gentleman with a taste for the Rubenesque. To be perfectly candid, I no longer tour this region. I play the larger markets, but they're remodeling my winter home. This is just a last-minute something to avoid the dust. What brings *you* to this shithole?"

Alice leaned back on her elbows. "I was heading to Seattle to see my family but my husband cancelled my credit card."

Ruth's eyes roamed Alice's body. "Why'd he do that?"

"I guess cause I left a note saying I was leaving him."

"Oh baby, that was a tactical error. This is why I always say girls gotta make their own money. Can your family help you?"

Alice sighed.

Ruth laughed. "You didn't tell 'em."

Alice sucked on the joint and sank deeper into the mattress. "I got a job around the corner, working for this lady who sells arts and crafts . . ."

"I know that bitch." Ruth sat up and flipped the cassette. "How come you never told them?"

"I spent the last thirteen years telling them how great things were."

"And they weren't."

"I mean, I had a good life."

"Is that your silver car in the parking lot?"

"Yeah."

"So, what's the problem?"

Alice shook her head. "You ever feel like you just wasted your life?"

"No. Uh-uh."

"I don't know if leaving him was the smartest thing I ever did, or the dumbest. I honestly don't. I have no idea what I'm going to do. I'm broke. I don't know what I'm going to do with the rest of my life. And, it wasn't bad, my marriage. Nothing was bad. I just never felt . . . like his wife."

"So, clearly this is a rich dude we're talking about."

"He does okay."

"Like a doctor? What? A bond trader or something?"

"Actually he's a musician."

"Musician? Hell, what musician is loaded?" Ruth stared at her fingernails. "Is he someone I heard of?"

"I don't know. Chick Wolfson?"

"Bullshit!" Ruth stared at Alice. And then she laughed, a barking wallop. "That's your husband? I love that prick."

"Well, he's all yours."

"Why the hell did you leave? Was he cheating?"

"No. I don't know. I doubt it."

"Then, what?"

"I don't think I love him."

Ruth laughed again. "Who gives a shit? He's rich for Christ sake. And he's okay looking. A little skinny."

"I felt like I was dying."

"Oh, well then. So now here you are in paradise. How do you like living in this shit box, working for that bitch in her velour tracksuit? I swear, I never met anyone like you."

"I just have a few dollars left. I asked Joyce if she'd give me an advance, but she won't do it."

Ruth took another long pull on the joint. "You just gotta hang in."

"You wouldn't be able to lend me something for a couple of days, would you? I can pay you back on Friday."

Ruth coughed. She tilted her head forward, staring up at Alice from the floor.

"Forget it," said Alice. "Forget I asked."

Ruth took another drag on the joint.

Alice sat up and put her feet on the floor. "I should go to bed."

"Why? Cause I'm not giving you money?"

Alice reached for the doorknob. "No, cause I'm tired."

"Where you from in Seattle?"

"What does that have to do with anything?"

"Just, where you from?"

"Look, I'm broke, all right? I signed a prenup. I never wanted his money. I don't want anything from anybody. I'm not hitting up my folks. You have no idea who I am."

"It's just a simple question."

"No, it's not. I can tell by looking at you that you got all sorts of ideas about who I am and you don't know the first thing about me," she said. "Bellevue. All right? You happy now?"

Ruth nodded. "Where all the dentists and judges live."

"Yup. That's right." She opened the door.

"Oh well, la di da. Why don't you call one of them?"

Alice was silent.

"You want some quick cash?" asked Ruth. "There's a bar across the street. Lotta guys over there'd be happy to help you out for a little favor."

"That's gross. Good night," said Alice.

"That's why you knocked on my door, ain't it?"

"I would have paid you back."

"We all got a rap, sweetheart. I know how it works. Go back to your rock star, you rich bitch."

Alice slammed the door. Across the hall, Percy peeked out. Alice glared at him and ducked into her room, locking the door behind her.

15

She lay in bed listening to Ruth storm around her room. A door slammed and she heard footsteps recede down the hall.

She went to the window and watched Ruth emerge from the hotel in a long coat over sweat pants and red pumps. The woman staggered like a bear toward a group of men who stood under the awning of the Pastime. A huge man in a down vest stretched out his arms and gave her a kiss. The other men laughed as he grabbed her ass and pretended to bite her neck. Ruth pushed him away.

The steady pounding of rain drowned out their voices but Alice continued watching. After a few minutes the other men went back inside, leaving the huge man alone with Ruth. She touched his cheek and he pushed it away. He asked her something. He looked around, then pulled bills from his wallet. She stuffed the money in her pocket and they vanished into the alley.

Alice watched the raindrops hit the window. They clung to

the glass for a moment then slid quickly to the ledge. Ruth and the man emerged from the darkness. He went back into the bar and she crossed the street to the hotel. Alice closed the curtain. She listened to Ruth's footsteps climb the stairs and walk back to her room.

*   *   *

Alice awoke early. The room seemed bleaker in the morning light. Aside from the peeling particleboard table and a floor lamp with a dented shade, her bed was the only piece of furniture in the room. When she stood she noticed a folded newspaper under her door. She grabbed it and bills fluttered to the floor. One hundred dollars. She snatched the bills and stuffed them into her purse.

She tiptoed past Ruth's room, and down the hall. The lobby was empty. Milo still had her watch. She went to the desk and tried to pull the drawer open but it was locked. Keep it, she thought.

A couple of blocks from the hotel she stopped at a Chevron station and had her tank filled. The rain fell hard as she drove past the lumber mill. Pressing on the gas, she rounded a bend thick with fir trees. She approached the overpass and began to slow down. She approached the northbound sign and was about to pass it when she stopped. A logging truck honked its horn but she found herself unable to move. "Which way, Alice?" she asked herself. She kept seeing the image of Ruth crossing the street in her red pumps. When she'd said that she'd pay her back, she'd meant it. So, why was she here? And what did this have to do with her leaving Chick, and with marrying him, and with lying to her folks that she was in love? It all seemed connected, but she didn't know how. She sat stopped on the overpass. If she headed south she knew that despite whatever Chick said to her, it would be too easy to go back to him. She could feel her will weakening. Together they'd pretend that nothing had happened, and eventually he'd tease her about the time she left him for forty-eight hours and it would become a story that they told their friends, the story about poor Chick Wolfson and his high-strung, mercurial wife. Everyone would laugh and slap the table. Or, she could drive north to Seattle and stay with her folks. But she could feel it from them as well, this push to go back to him. Her family was not a refuge. She could feel an anger rising inside of her, giving voice to something she couldn't articulate. This is your chance, the voice said. She needed something, but she didn't know what it was. She needed some ground under her feet, a reason, something to convince her that she would not go back to him.

The logging truck hit its blinker and moved slowly around her. She sat parked on the bridge, fists of rain landing hard on her roof. The highway traffic beneath her was a blur. She spoke to herself. "North or south, Alice?"

She hit her signal.

She did a U-turn, and drove back into town.

16

A lice trudged up the hill to work.

Joyce smiled effusively when she entered. "Cliff Shoemaker's son came in this morning. His old man died last week and left some fine appliances. They're a mess, but making 'em pretty's where the profit is."

Trudy was on her knees scrubbing the inside of a fridge. Alice pulled a sponge from the bucket and got to work next to her. Trudy blew a lock of hair from her cheek and told Alice, "Lester dresses up as Santa every Christmas for the pre-schoolers."

"That's interesting," said Alice.

"He has his own suit."

* * *

Webb kept glancing out the window, hoping to see her again. He thought about the way she looked at him when he fixed her lock. He was standing on a stepladder, moving gallon cans of apple juice from the top shelf to a lower one, when

George crept behind him. "What are you doing?"

"The cans are too high," he said. "Folks can't reach 'em."

"Put 'em back."

"They could hurt someone if they fall."

The old man smashed his cane against the base of the stepladder. Webb moved the cans back to where they'd been. He glanced out the window.

"Whattya keep looking out there for? She ain't looking for you."

* * *

At lunchtime Alice entered wearing black pants and a black sweater. As Webb finished serving a customer, he heard the squeak of the metal door and the clack of his boss's cane on the floor. "How's that lock working?" George asked Alice.

"It's fine," she said. "I was just coming in to thank you both."

"Let me know if there's anything else you need." George winked at her with his one rheumy eye. He turned to Webb. "Cooley, why don't you go back there and open up them boxes?"

Alice reached into the cooler next to the cash register and removed a sandwich.

"That means now."

"I'll just ring her up," said Webb.

George walked around the counter. "I'll take care of her." He passed Alice. "If he bothers you, you let me know."

"He's not bothering me," she said.

"Bothers me plenty," said George.

Webb walked back to the stock room.

"This it?" asked George, scanning her sandwich.

"Yes."

He removed a pack of American Spirits from his pocket

and studied her as she walked to the door. He turned to see Webb watching him from the stockroom. He lit his cigarette and waved out the match.

17

Webb stood at the window of his apartment, drying a bowl and staring down at the street. The dish had been dry for over an hour, but he continued to run the cloth around in circles, feeling the smoothness of the plastic. He'd lost track of time when he saw Alice cross the street and walk into Corky's. He pulled a novel from his shelf and lay down. He tried to read, but he couldn't see the words.

He opened his closet door and removed his suit. His shoes were cracked from the rain. Before he had time to tell himself it was a bad idea he was already outside. He slowed as he passed the tavern. He listened to the voices, but kept walking.

He pushed open the front door. She sat at the counter talking to the waitress. He paused for a moment before walking to a booth at the back. He pretended to study the menu. When she turned, he smiled. She smiled back. He walked over and took a seat on the stool next to her.

"I didn't see you come in," she said.

The waitress held a pot and asked if he wanted a cup of

coffee. "Thank you," he said. He suddenly felt ridiculous in his suit.

It surprised him that his hand was steady when he lifted the cup. He wondered if his past was visible to her, if she could see in his eyes what almost everyone in town already knew. He wondered if it was deception to not simply blurt out his sins to her.

"Where're you coming from?"

He glanced down at his tie and shrugged. "Nowhere. It's just . . . laundry day."

She laughed. He made her laugh. He remembered how the girls used to look at him when he was younger. They would swoon, and he would look at them in bewilderment, wondering what the hell they were seeing.

"Is your boss always so rude?"

"I don't take it personal."

The waitress placed Alice's dinner on the table.

Webb didn't see Lester appear until Alice looked up and greeted him.

"Hi there," said Lester. "Am I interrupting?"

"No," said Alice. "I don't think so."

Webb forced himself to meet Lester's gaze. Lester winked at him.

"Do you guys know each other?" asked Alice.

"Sure," said Lester. "How you doing, Webb?" He shook his hand and sat down next to Alice. He leaned forward, chewing a wad of gum. "George treating you okay?"

Webb nodded.

"He seems like a piece of work," said Alice.

"George?" Lester laughed. He blew a bubble and made it snap inside his mouth. "He's a curmudgeon, but he's harmless, wouldn't you say, Webb?"

Webb tried to smile, but he couldn't.

"How are you liking it here?" Lester asked Alice.

"I don't know yet."

Webb sat quietly. They were talking about gum. Lester said something about his "disgusting habit" and how he had just quit smoking. Webb forced himself to hold Lester's gaze. He tried to listen, but his brain was full of noise. He waited for Lester to say something that would give him away. He waited for Alice to be charmed by Lester. He waited for his life to go back to where it was before.

And then, suddenly, Ned Feeney, entered the restaurant. Lester excused himself. "Better go talk to my client," he said. He touched Alice's arm. "Nice seeing you again." He hit Webb on the shoulder, and then joined Ned at a booth.

Alice turned to him.

"I better get going," said Webb.

"Are you okay?"

He pulled out his wallet.

"Don't you want to finish your coffee?" She looked at him strangely. "Let me get this," she said.

"No, I . . ."

"I got it," she said.

"I'll get the next one," he said.

"I'd like that." She smiled.

He walked out of the restaurant. She watched Lester watch him from the booth over Ned Feeney's shoulder.

18

Alice paid her bill and waved to Lester. He mimed for her to call him. She walked across the street and entered the hotel.

She put her key into the lock. As she opened her door, Ruth shoved her head into the hallway. "How was your second day in paradise? Magical, ain't it?"

"Thanks for helping me out," said Alice. "I'm going to pay you back."

"Forget it," said Ruth. "We all been in the gutter once."

"I get paid Friday."

Ruth waved a hand. "Whenever," she said. "I'm gonna have some herb. Care to join me?"

"I can't. I have to take care of some things." Alice went into her room. She removed her cell phone from her suitcase. There were fourteen messages from her mother. Alice listened to the first one. Her mother sounded panicked. She deleted the messages and lay on her bed. She typed a text:

Mom. I'm taking a break from
Chick. I'm staying with friends.
Everything is fine.
I'll call you soon. Love, Alice

A moment later, her phone rang. "Hi Mom."

"Where are you?"

"I'm in Oregon."

"What are you doing in Oregon?"

"I'm staying with friends."

"What friends do you have in Oregon?"

"You don't know them." She could lie in generalities to her mother, but could not bring herself to invent fictional friends. "I just needed to get away."

"What happened? Did something happen?"

"No. Everything's okay."

"Did he cheat on you? Honey, I want you to know you can tell me anything. We're here for you."

"No, mom. It's nothing like that."

"Then why are you doing this? Is he gay? And sweetheart, if you're not comfortable talking about it . . ."

"He's not gay."

"Then tell me. I have people praying for you."

"I don't know if I'm in love with him, okay?"

There was silence. She could hear her mother thinking. "Alice, you've been married a long time. Trust me, you're in love with him. Things change. Love doesn't always feel the same. You can't make snap decisions when it comes to a marriage."

"It's not a snap decision, Mom, and no offense, but I'm not sure I want your advice on this. And you know what? I'm not sure I need your prayers. At least, please tell them to stop praying that we get back together. I don't think that's a good prayer, and besides, I don't think God likes being told what to do."

"What prayer do you want then?"

"I don't know. This is embarrassing. I wish you hadn't told your prayer group. I'm going to be thirty-seven."

"You have not wasted your life."

"What? Who said I had?"

"I know you, Alice. I know what you're thinking. You're too hard on yourself. You're a good person. You've built a nice life with Chick."

"I haven't done anything."

"You're a good wife."

"Are you upset that you don't have grandchildren?"

"What mother wouldn't be?"

"That's what I thought you'd say."

"Sweetheart, part of being a parent is learning to cope with disappointment."

"Wow."

"I'm not saying we're disappointed in you. We're so impressed with the life you've created, and the way you conduct yourself. Would it be nice to have grandchildren? Of course it would. But maybe that's not God's plan for us."

"What did I create? I married a successful musician."

"Honey, I'm not sure what the problem is."

"Me neither."

"You can still go back to him. Just get in your car. He wants you back."

"You talked to him?"

"We were worried."

"Wait. You *both* talked to him?"

"Your father did most of the talking."

"What did he say?"

"Who, your father? Nothing. He told him stories."

"Stories?"

"Like when you were a kid and you told the teacher you were going to sit where you wanted."

"Oh, I see. Dad told him that I was stubborn."

"He didn't say stubborn. I listened to the whole thing."

Alice could feel the fury building inside her. "Mom. Did Dad apologize for me leaving?"

"Apologize? No. Sort of. Darling, he was looking out for you."

Alice hung up.

She went into the hall and knocked on Ruth's door.

Ruth held a cup of wine in one hand and a joint in the other. "Siddown." She handed the joint to Alice and sat back at the table. Alice took a long puff and closed her eyes. Her body sank into the mattress.

A car honked outside. Ruth went to the window. "Yeah, I'm coming Ricky, hold your horses." She pulled her raincoat from the closet. "Honey, I gotta go."

Alice grinned.

"Damn, you're buzzin.'" Ruth put out a hand and helped Alice to her feet. She steadied her as they went out the door. Ruth squeezed Alice's shoulders. "You're gonna be okay, kid." She clomped down the hallway.

"Hey," said Alice, "Wanna get breakfast tomorrow?"

"Try me in the morning," said Ruth, and disappeared down the stairs.

* * *

Webb lay in bed, playing her words over. "I'd like that," she'd said. He turned on his side and wondered how long it would be before she learned the truth. He turned again, but his past rolled with him, following him. He thought that twenty years of incarceration had silenced his desires, but it hadn't. The adult magazines that were passed around were not for him. He had willed that part of himself to sleep, but now, when he thought of her, he could feel something inside of him awakening.

He fell into a twisted sleep fighting with the possibility that he could be a man sitting with a woman, drinking a cup of coffee.

19

Alice sat in a corner booth at Corky's watching Ruth dig into the trucker's special.

"I remember this one poor bastard, he had no hands," said Ruth, waving her fork in the air. "Wanted to know if he could give me oral." Ruth had a voice that carried. "I said I'm a dominatrix, I ain't desperate. Besides, your tongue ain't the whole world."

The restaurant was filling with customers. Lester waited at the front door behind a group of mill workers who stood with their hands plunged into their pockets. His eyes scanned the restaurant, and when he saw Alice his eyebrows arced. His face broke into a look of sudden relief. Alice watched as he shoved past the men and made his way toward her table.

"Look at that," said Ruth. "The old dog already sniffed you out."

"How do you know Lester?" asked Alice.

"Who doesn't? He's the grand poobah of Waiden. And a prolific cocksman according to local legend."

Lester stopped at their table. He placed a hand on Alice's shoulder and turned to Ruth. "How you doing? I'm Lester," he said. He stuck out his other hand to shake hers, but she offered him her fingertips. "Okay," he said, playing along. He turned to Alice. "What are you doing for lunch today? I know you said you can't get dinner, but lunch is different, right? I mean, what kind of mischief can we get up to during daylight hours?"

"I'm sorry, but I still can't," said Alice.

"This is a goddamn married woman, you home wrecker," said Ruth. She dug a chunk of pancake from her gum with a fingernail. "But you can pay for our breakfast if you like."

"It's just lunch," said Lester.

"Sorry," said Alice.

"Well…" Lester glanced around the restaurant, bewildered. "I tried," he said.

20

A yellow-haired kid with a sneer and the faintest down over his top lip entered the store with two buddies trailing. His jeans were soiled and his T-shirt was ripped up the side. His greasy hair fell over his eyes. Six months earlier he came in and bought a soda. While Webb rang him up, the kid said, "Everyone in town talks about what you did." Webb had just stared at him. Frozen. He could smell him from across the counter. He smelled like sour milk. The kid smirked. There was elation in his eyes, a predatory leer that said he'd bagged his quarry.

"Is it true?" the kid had asked.

Webb was silent.

One of the kid's pals had looked over, eyes bulging. "Hell, Trevor, come on."

But Trevor didn't move. He stared at Webb, holding his gaze. "I heard you smashed your wife's head in with an iron," he said. "Is that what you did?"

Webb had felt the nausea rise up his windpipe. He thought

he was suffocating. None of his defenses worked. He could take care of himself with men, with bullies, maniacs and psychos, but he never anticipated being brought to his knees by some kid who had barely entered puberty.

Webb nodded. "Yeah," he said. "That's what I did." And when the words left him, he felt himself shrinking into the floor, until there was nothing left of him but rage pressing out from inside his veins.

Trevor came in every few weeks after that. He came in alone, or with his buddies. He'd say, "How's it hanging, killer?" or, "Done any ironing lately?"

The three boys stalked the aisles, making noises and cursing each other. Webb glanced at the stock room pretending to busy himself.

George stormed up the aisle. "Get yourselves goin'!"

"We didn't do nothin'," said Trevor.

"Get outta here." George slashed the air with his cane.

Webb recognized the look in Trevor's eyes, the delirious thrill as he chewed his bottom lip and walked toward the old man inviting him to strike. "What are you gonna do, hit me?" George's eyes bugged. He waved his cane and Trevor jerked back. "You dumb old bastard." Trevor pulled a shelf down and some cereal boxes fell to the floor.

"Pick 'em up," said George.

"Maybe I'll call the cops on you," said Trevor. "Assault and battery."

"Come back and I'll kill you."

The other two boys ran out of the store. Trevor backed up and kicked the bucket that held the umbrellas before shoving on the door. He went outside and crossed in front of the window, raised a middle finger and patted his jacket pocket bulging with contraband.

"Get 'em," said George.

Webb climbed slowly down the stepladder. He jogged half-heartedly to the door. Once outside, he stopped and watched the boys run down the hill. Trevor turned back and raised his finger again while his buddies sprinted past the bank and vanished around the corner. He strolled backwards in lazy steps, digging a candy bar from his pocket. He unwrapped it and bit into the end, chewing with exaggerated bites.

An hour later, Mike Shute's carpentry van pulled up in front of the store. Shute ran the only full-time carpentry business in town. He nodded to Webb and continued toward the stock room, his apprentice, Dez, following. George shook Shute's hand and said something about "the goddamn little thieves." Webb caught a glimpse of Mike snapping open his measuring tape and calling out figures to Dez who scribbled the information onto a pad. They left and returned after lunch with a stack of lumber.

Webb walked back to the stock room to get more fresh corn for one of the bins. They were building a landing against the interior wall of the stock room. Shute cut and framed a square-foot space in the wall.

Later, Dale Grimes arrived and installed a shiny black one-way mirror allowing George visual access to his store from the back room. At five o'clock George got the workers and Webb to carry his desk up the six steps. Returning to the cash register, Webb could see the faint outline of his boss watching him from behind the dark glass.

21

Alice was stacking fabric on a shelf when Joyce placed a hand at the base of her back.

"We need to talk."

She guided Alice to the back room.

"This is a small town," said Joyce.

Joyce wore a lime terry-cloth tracksuit.

"We're not some big city where everyone does whatever they want and nobody notices." She made a cracking sound with her jaw.

"What happened?"

"My employees don't eat with whores." She smiled stiffly.

"Pardon me?"

Joyce's eyelids fluttered, "And you shouldn't be living in that place. I'll ask one of the ladies if they know of any rooms for rent. Now go finish folding, then get back to those buttons."

Alice reentered the store. She watched Joyce chat merrily about hemlines and hairdos with the women who had begun to trickle in for their morning of knitting. The room grew loud with conversation while hands busily crafted scarves and baby wear. Alice sat in the circle with a large basket in her lap, separating buttons and placing them into small, clear plastic boxes. As she listened, she began to hear the underlying rhythms of something tribal, a high court for the town's distaff elders. The conversation moved through an informal agenda of daily grievances as they arrived at a consensus on how things ought to be. Feathers were ruffled and smoothed again, all with eyes cast downward on their needles. At some point, the conversation turned to Ruth. "She tried to come in here once, didn't she?"

Joyce rolled her eyes. "She wanted to make bracelets. I told her she could buy what she needed, but she couldn't stay."

"She's strange-looking," said a woman. "What happened to her? Did she get beat with the ugly stick?"

"Evelyn, you're bad."

"She strips at that skanky Misty's place."

"Only when she's not turning tricks in the alley."

"Ugh."

"Alice, didn't I see you having breakfast with her?"

The women stopped sewing.

"She didn't know," said Joyce. "She's staying across the street right now, can you imagine? But you're moving out this week, aren't you?"

"Yes."

"I heard Kate Zelevansky's renting a room, but not till November."

"Alice needs to move out right away," said Joyce.

22

Gates Pharmacy was the last storefront at the top of the hill. Gene Gates noticed Webb Cooley cross in front of his place twice that morning. He glanced in the window and then walked on. He was eating a sandwich at the counter when Webb pushed open the door.

"Can I help you?" asked Gene. He didn't say Webb's name, though they knew each other since they were kids.

Webb spoke softly. "Just need some stuff."

"How's business down there?" asked Gene.

"Good." Webb laid a tube of toothpaste in his basket and continued down the aisle. He dropped in a toothbrush and a box of razor blades. As he walked toward Gene, he kept his eyes down. He stood in front of the condoms, staring at his choices. He wished Gene would keep talking. He tried to think of something to say, but couldn't. "How's business for *you*?"

"Slow," said Gene. Webb dropped a three-pack of condoms into his basket and approached the counter.

"I guess it'd be too much to hope for some sun today," said Gene.

He rang up each of Webb's purchases. He picked up the box of condoms and punched in the price. "Total's twenty-six twelve." Webb looked up. "It's the razor blades. God knows why they cost so much. Guess cause they know we need 'em."

Gene gave him his change and put his purchases into a bag.

Webb pushed open the door and walked outside. He sucked in the cold air, his heart thumped in his chest.

23

A lice sat alone at the counter of Corky's eating a turkey dinner. It was quiet. While she ate, Lester pushed open the front door.

"Don't worry," he said. "I'm not gonna ask you out." He sat down heavily next to her. He gave the waitress a tired smile. "Phyllis, I need a beer."

"You okay?" asked Alice.

"Fine," he said. He jerked his head. "I just have a client who can't keep his mouth shut. That guy I've been talking to . . . Ned Feeney. Today the son-of-a-bitch called the plaintiff a *wetback*."

"Uh oh."

"Judge fined him three hundred bucks, so he called the judge an *A-hole* for another three hundred, and now what could have been a simple plea bargain has become my nightmare."

Phyllis placed a beer in front of him.

"That sucks."

"What sucks is that my client is broke, and now that it's gone to trial it's become a huge waste of my time," he said.

"Sorry, I'm just having a lousy day. Aren't you glad you let me sit down?" He took a swig of his beer and stared out the window. "How's Estrogen Central?"

Alice laughed. "I got scolded today for having breakfast with Ruth."

"You better watch it," he said. "Those women run this town."

"Clearly."

"I don't get why you're up here. I mean, look at you. Why would you want to leave San Francisco?"

She smiled. "It's complicated."

"A woman of secrets," he said. He had a look in his eyes, like he was impossibly attracted to her. "I just think there must be a million opportunities down there."

"Sure," she said. "If you've got a law degree . . . or clean up houses after they're foreclosed on."

"That's the one thing about this place," he said. "Not exactly a lot of room for advancement. I've sort of hit the glass ceiling."

"Why'd you come back?" she asked. "I imagine you could have gone anywhere."

"My father was getting ready to retire, and I took over. My classmates were all working 80-hour weeks, articling with big firms for no pay and I walked into an instant practice. It's small-time, sure, and I gotta do a bit of everything, estate planning, personal injury, you name it, but it's a decent living." He stared at his hands. "I told myself I'd do it for a while, and a while turned into this."

They sat in silence, listening to the rain.

"So, what are you doing over there?" he asked, pointing to the scarred metal door of the Frontier Hotel.

"I'm broke, like Ned," she said.

"No, you're not." He smiled. "You're a long way from broke.

Something tells me you're not planning on staying too long."

She studied him, pondering how much to reveal.

"C'mon, I'm your lawyer," he said. "Attorney-client privilege. You're waiting for something. I'm not sure what it is, but I know that look. Did you have a fight with your husband?"

"A fight? No, uh-uh," she said. "He refuses to fight."

"Ohh," he said. "You don't want to go back, but you're afraid you might."

She looked at him, surprised. "How did you know that?"

"Cause that's every relationship I've ever been in," he said. "I can't stay, but I don't want to be alone."

"That's awfully candid of you. And sort of sad."

"And pretty common."

"You sound like an expert."

"In bad relationships? I am."

"So, what's the answer?"

"If you're asking my opinion, you gotta keep going forward. You can't go back."

"But how do I know if I'm running away, or if I'm leaving a legitimately bad situation? What if I just repeat this whole thing with someone else?"

"Right," he said. "That's the big question. When is it escape, and when is it self-preservation? Well, first off, it's not about him. You're only running away if you haven't learned the lesson. Once you figure out the lesson, you can leave, and if you really want to, you can always go back."

"You sound terribly wise."

"Don't confuse insight with wisdom."

"What's the difference?"

"Wisdom is acting on your insights."

"That's a good point," she said, eating her mashed potatoes. "So how long do you figure it'll take me to learn my lesson?"

"Depends. Do you love him?"

She stared at her food. "I wish I knew how to answer that. I thought I did. There're days I'm convinced I never loved him, and others when I think I must have . . . otherwise why did I stay so long?"

"Why did you marry him?"

She moved her food around the plate with her fork. "I was young and smitten and I was going to have him, dammit. It was not a well-planned decision," she said. "Are you divorced?"

He nodded. "Twice."

"Everyone I know either pretends things are better than they are, and then one day it's over, or they blame their spouse for everything and stay married fifty years."

He cleared his throat. "So, you're hiding out."

"I guess I am."

He sipped his beer. "That makes two of us."

"Don't worry," she said. "I won't blow your cover."

"It's just nice talking to someone who knows I *have* a cover. Hey, if you don't go back to him, *I'll* marry you."

"Well, thanks," she said. She put her fork down. "You're very charitable."

"That was a stupid thing to say."

"Don't worry about it."

"Weird thing is, I think I might have meant it."

"I don't know whether that's a compliment or if you've just run out of women here."

"Both," he said, and swigged his beer. "Just put it in your hat."

"I'll do that." She opened her purse and placed some cash on the counter. "I need to go to sleep."

"You gotta get out of that place," he said, pointing across the street at the Frontier.

"I know," she said.

*   *   *

Alice lay in bed and was awakened by the sound of tapping at her door.

"Alice?" Ruth's voice sounded fragile.

She held her breath and listened to the methodical drumming of rain against the window.

She heard a door open down the hall. "Percy, get lost," Ruth hissed.

Alice lay still, remembering what Joyce had said about staying away from Ruth. There was another tap at the door. Alice tried to breathe as quietly as possible. After a few minutes she heard Ruth's footsteps retreat and the click of her door shutting. Alice exhaled deeply. She listened to Ruth's drawers open and close, and the sounds of her getting undressed. She didn't play music, but she hummed to herself as she prepared for bed. With each footstep the floor shifted. In the bathroom, the faucet squeaked. Ruth blew her nose, a terrible honking noise followed by several great sighs. There were grunts and groans and a long silence following by the sound of a toilet flushing, and then she went back into her bedroom and shut the door.

After a few minutes there were no sounds at all, except for the rain against the window.

24

George stuck his head out from the stock room and motioned to Webb with his cane. "Get in here."

He sat at his desk, eyes fixed on the adding machine. "We're missing seventy-three dollars and sixteen cents."

"I didn't take your money," said Webb. The front bell sounded as a customer entered. George snapped an envelope off his desk and threw it at Webb, hitting him in the chest. Webb picked the envelope off the floor. He opened it and removed the check. "This isn't the correct amount."

"I took it out of your pay."

"I told you I didn't take your money."

"Tell it to Tripp."

Webb folded the check and shoved it in his pocket before returning to the counter to help the customer.

* * *

He swept the front of the store. The parcel of cod he bought from George sat on the counter.

"What are you still doing here?" George stood at the back in his raincoat.

"Cleaning up."

"Let's go."

Webb climbed the sidewalk as slowly as possible, hoping to see her round the corner at the top of the hill. He reached his door and waited a minute before going inside. He climbed the stairs, but then something stopped him. He went back out and stood in the rain. Ten minutes later she rounded the corner. She saw him and crossed the street.

"You're getting wet," she said.

He held up his parcel. "I was just gonna cook some fish. Would you like to join me?"

Across the street, men stood outside the Pastime watching him as he opened the door and let the woman inside.

She climbed the stairs ahead of him. She was aware of him walking behind her, and she wondered if he was staring at her butt. When she reached the top, she glanced back to see his eyes downcast watching the steps in front of him. He brushed past her and pulled a set of keys from his pocket. They stood in the small square hallway to his apartment.

He opened the door. "Come on in," he said.

She entered.

He went to the sink and unwrapped the fish. "You can put your coat on the chair."

"It's wet. I don't want to ruin the wood. Can I put it in here?" she asked.

"Sure."

She opened the bathroom door and laid it over the tub. She walked back into the room. It smelled of worn paperbacks and lemon cleaner. A double bed sat in the middle of the room, a wool army blanket tucked tightly under the mattress without a crease. The bed looked small compared to the California king she shared with Chick, and for a second she imagined herself lying in it, sharing it with Webb, their bodies pressed tightly together. She felt her face grow hot. In the corner next to the window was a bookcase filled with paperbacks, and on his side table was a stack of novels.

"How long have you lived here?" she asked.

"Eight months," he said. "I grew up down the road." He removed a cookie sheet from his cupboard. He tore off a strip of silver foil and placed it on the sheet.

She studied the photograph on top of his dresser of a young boy and girl sitting on a couch.

"My sister's kids."

She put the photo back on the dresser. "Do you know that guy, Percy, across the hall from me?"

He laid the fish on the silver foil. "Yeah, I do."

"Was he really a friend of yours?"

"Years ago. He wasn't always like that." He took a clove of garlic and smashed it with the side of a wide knife, separating it from the chaff.

"What happened to him?"

"He was a choker for the mill, tied chains around the trees after they were felled. Chain caught his sleeve and snapped his arm at the elbow. Now he lives off disability."

"No," she said. "I mean, what happened to him?"

Webb looked at her, pondering this. "I guess he gave up." He mixed olive oil into a glass with the garlic, and then squeezed a lemon over it.

"He's scary."

He ground pepper into the glass, then added salt. "Yeah, I understand. I don't think he's dangerous. I don't. But if he does anything, or says anything, just let me know. Or you can talk to Milo." He spooned the mixture over the fish, then closed the foil and slid the pan into the oven.

Alice stared at the small pencil sketches of the coastline drawn on typing paper and taped to his wall. Each drawing was from a different vantage point, with the same long, dark rock jutting out from the shoreline.

"Did you do these?"

"I used to fish off that rock when I was a kid," he said. He gazed at her from behind. She wore a navy skirt and thin beige sweater over a white cotton shirt. He could smell her soap, faint after a day of work. He wanted to touch her, feel the smoothness of her skin. She stared at the drawings, but she could feel his eyes on her. She wanted to turn to him, but she didn't move. She just stood there, feeling his presence.

"I've never gone fishing," she said. Her voice was soft.

"That's a good spot for pole fishing. The fish like it there, mostly surf perch. Can't get 'em in the store cause they're too close to shore for the commercial boats. Water's smashing all around, but in that pocket the water's shallow and still enough that they're safe from most predators. Except me, I guess."

She closed her eyes, listening to the low rumble in his voice. Her body tingled, and she felt suddenly caught, embarrassed. Something told her she should leave, but instead, she turned to face him. His eyes were silver.

"I hope you don't mind, I don't have any wine," he said.

"I don't need any wine," she said.

He took some lettuce from the fridge. She stood next to him at the counter and helped him make a salad. They worked silently.

He opened the oven.

"Smells good," she said.

He removed the fish and cut it in two.

"I don't usually have guests," he said. He bent over and picked up his solid oak desk against the wall, and carried it to the edge of the bed. He placed the chair on one side, "You can sit here," he said.

She sat down, and he sat on the edge of the bed. She took a bite of fish. "Mmmm, delicious," she said. She looked up to see his eyes were closed and his face was tilted over the food. She stopped eating and waited for him to finish his prayer.

"How did you learn to cook so well?"

"I used to cook for my little sister."

"Does your family still live here?"

"My mother died. My sister, Shelly, lives a couple miles down the road. She remarried a few years ago, but I don't see her much these days."

"How come?"

"I don't think her husband likes me. She was married to another fella for a few years, a guy named Don, he seemed decent enough, but I guess it didn't take."

"Have you ever been married?"

"Yeah. Once," he said.

"What happened?"

He stared at his plate.

"Didn't take?" she asked.

He smiled. He cut a piece of fish with his fork and pushed it into his mouth.

They ate in silence.

She studied him, his brush cut, his silver eyes and sharp jaw. He ate slowly, methodically, tasting each bite. She realized she'd finished her plate, and suddenly felt nervous, exposed. "This is nice," she said. "If I'd known, I would have brought dessert."

"I have a mango and some vanilla ice cream."

"You thought of everything."

He continued eating, and she tried to think of something to say to avoid the quiet. She looked again at his sketches. "You're a good draftsman. Did you study somewhere?"

"No," he said. "I taught myself."

"I went to art school with folks who don't draw that well," she said.

"Thanks," he said.

He smiled, and suddenly Alice felt panicked. What was she doing here? She wanted to blurt out that she was married, but she didn't want to be rude. She wanted to put up a wall between them. Her brain was crowding with noise.

"Can I help you with the dishes?" she said.

"No. That's okay. I'll do them later."

"Well . . ." She stood up. "I should probably go."

"Why? Don't you want dessert?"

"No," she said. "I . . . I better go." She put on her coat and walked to the door.

He stuffed his hands into his pockets.

She reached for the door handle. "I'd like to see that rock sometime," she said.

As she opened the door, he took her wrist. He pulled her to him and kissed her on the mouth. She closed her eyes, and for the briefest moment the dreads and anxieties of her life vanished and she lost herself in him.

Then she pulled away.

She opened the door and went into the hall. He stood at the door and watched her disappear around the corner. He listened to her footsteps descend the stairs.

He turned out the lights and watched from the window as she emerged onto the sidewalk. He watched her walk down the hill until he couldn't see her anymore.

25

The next morning, Webb stood in front of his bathroom mirror, knotting his tie. Before his release he'd worn a tie only twice: on his wedding day, and again on the day of his sentencing. For the past eight months, he wore one every second Monday morning when he visited his parole officer.

The sky was ash. Thready clouds stretched to the horizon. The air was clean and cold and the drying sidewalk smelled of salt. Alice stepped from the front door of the hotel and spotted him walking down the hill toward her. "You're looking spiffy," she said. "Is it still laundry day?"

"I have a meeting." He glanced at the pavement. "I hope it was okay that I . . ."

". . . kissed me?" she said, trying to make a joke.

"Yeah."

"It's okay, it's just that . . ." She felt her face burning. "Actually . . ." she hoped he'd help her out, finish her sentence, but he didn't. "I'm still . . . well, I'm separated," she said. "I left my husband a week ago. I came up here from San Francisco to kind of . . . I can't get involved with anyone right now. Not that that's what you're looking for . . . I shouldn't have taken off my ring, but I was just . . ."

"I'm sorry," he said.

"No. I just don't want to lead anyone on."

"I understand," he said. "Well, I guess I'll see you later."

"Okay," she said.

He turned. She watched him walk down the hill.

*   *   *

The Waiden Adult Corrections Facility was a low cinderblock building with gray mesh-wire windows that shared a parking lot with the police station. Formerly, it had been the electric building, but a few years back Waiden had splurged and built a modern plant up the street. Inside the front door was a cramped waiting room with three chairs and a Formica table with a stack of nature magazines. On a small counter was a silver bell and a Xeroxed sign that read:

PLEASE FILL OUT A MONTHLY REPORT AND
PAY YOUR SUPERVISION FEE BEFORE ASKING
TO SEE YOUR PROBATION OFFICER!!!!

Webb entered and said hello to the secretary, Ellen Dubois, a fifty-year-old marathon runner who sat behind the counter working on a computer. She greeted Webb before returning to her work.

He filled out his form. He was browsing through a magazine when Paul Childers, on probation for drunken mischief, slunk in and dropped into a chair. He was unshaven and smelled of onion rings and diesel.

"They keep you waitin'," he said, one leg flopped over the other, his body twisted like there was no way to get comfortable.

His acrylic sweater was frayed and pilling.

"Aren't you 12:15?" asked Webb.

"So what . . . they're gonna see you first."

Webb went back to his magazine. Paul filled out his form and pushed it back through the window. He remained standing, staring down at Webb. "I should leave."

"You're not gonna leave."

"Let 'em find me." He laughed.

"Bring it up with Tripp."

Paul sniffed. "She won't do nothin'. She's worse'n any guard."

"You never went to jail, Paul."

Paul sat back down. "How come you wear that suit? You think Tripp cares what you wear?"

"I reckon probably not."

"She might get inclinations. You hear about Ned Feeney?"

"Yup."

"Shoulda blown off that wetback's head." He undid his sneaker, and retied it. "What would you a done?"

"Leave 'em alone."

"You allow that, they steal your livelihood. Down there them drug lords, they cut your head off, other things too."

Webb glanced at the clock.

"Got a smoke?" asked Paul.

"Don't smoke."

"I can't quit," said Paul. He picked up a National Geographic and pretended to flip through it.

Ellen's phone buzzed. "Webb, that's you."

He went to the door.

"Might not be here when you come out," said Paul.

Ellen let Webb in. He walked down the hall to an open door where Jane Tripp, a squat woman with short, gray hair and plain features sat behind a large metal desk. An ivory scar ran from her ear to the bridge of her nose. A German Shepherd slept at her feet. Webb handed her his report and his twenty-five dollar supervision fee. He sat across from her on a hard wooden chair.

"How are you making out this week, Mr. Cooley?"

"Fine."

"Have you talked to your sister?"

"No."

"Do you think you might call her?"

"She doesn't want to hear from me."

"It's good to stay in touch with family," she said.

Webb nodded.

"How's it going at work?" she asked, her eyes never straying from his face.

Webb adjusted his tie. "It's fine."

"How are you getting along with your boss?"

"He thinks I'm stealing from him."

"What happened?" Her look was accusatory, and his mind searched for something to confess.

"He says there was money missing, so he took it out of my pay."

"How much did he say was missing?"

"Seventy-three dollars."

She wrote something down in her folder. "We tried very hard to find you this job, Mr. Cooley."

"What about the mill?"

"We've gone over this. As long as Earl Park is foreman, it's not going to happen. They don't want trouble."

"Maybe I could talk to him?"

"He doesn't want to talk to you."

Webb squeezed his hands in frustration. "Did he say that?"

"I called the mill. That's what he said."

"I want to know what he said exactly."

"That if the mill gave you a job he would . . . raise holy hell." Tripp reached down and patted her dog's head. "Mr. Cooley, you killed his sister."

Webb stared at the floor, like he was remembering. "You said something about a property manager position."

"They don't want an ex-con. The fact is, getting you a job here was not easy," she said. Webb stared at the floor. "Have you been drinking?"

Sometimes he wondered if he was lying when he told the truth. He was under suspicion for so long that he felt an impulse to confess rather than suffer the indignity of an inquisition. "No."

"You haven't been to the Pastime?"

He shook his head.

"You're not drinking at home?"

"I told you, I don't drink anymore."

She wrote something in her book. "Why does Mr. Plotki think you're stealing from him?"

He glanced at the narrow window covered with mesh-wire. "He doesn't trust anyone." Tripp nodded. The dog watched him with one eye open. "Can I ask you something?" he said. "I've been out for eight months now, working hard. I want permission to go to the coast."

"You know the rule, Mr. Cooley. Not outside the city limits for the first year." She continued filling out her paperwork. "I want to speak to your boss about this stealing business."

"There is no stealing business." Webb dug a knuckle into the bone above his eye. "He just doesn't want to pay me."

"What are your plans for the next two weeks?"

"Work. Go home. Read." He shrugged.

"Have you thought about what we discussed?" she asked. "Starting a hobby?"

He tapped his finger against his leg. On the wall was a framed photograph of a couple Webb presumed to be Tripp's parents; a small, round couple planted unsmiling in front of a redwood. "Maybe I'll take up stamp collecting."

"That sounds like an excellent idea," she said. "I'll see you in two weeks, Mr. Cooley."

Webb stood slowly and stopped at the door. The German Shepherd emitted a low growl. "You have authority to give travel permits out of state," he said.

"Mr. Cooley, unless you have a legitimate reason for leaving the city limits, it is my job to enforce the court's decision. Please close the door on your way out."

"That's not what I'm asking."

The dog's ears pricked up. He watched Webb through cold black eyes.

"I want to know why you won't let me?"

"Mr. Cooley . . ."

"I don't lie," he said. "I'm not a liar."

"Mr. Cooley, please don't interrupt me again. Whether you realize it or not, I am working on your behalf. This decision was not made in haste. It was made with the best interests of you and the community in mind. If you fail to see your parole as a privilege, the board will be more than happy to un-grant it, and have you serve out the remainder of your term back at OSP."

Webb walked back down the hall.

"Still here," said Paul, grinning. Webb pushed open the metal door and walked out into the soft rain.

26

He crossed the parking lot and stepped over the cement curb to the street. Behind him, he heard his name. He turned to see Officer John Smith jogging toward him. John was a few years younger than Webb. His uniform hung loosely off his bony frame. His hair was prematurely gray, almost white. He had a long narrow face with small angry eyes and a hawkish nose, but when he spoke it was an earnest voice, soft and childlike. John was gentle and got into police work for all the right reasons. He called himself a peace officer, and as a result commanded little respect. He was too tall and too thin to exert much influence, and when he moved beyond a trot, his elbows flew ridiculously from his sides and his knees smashed together, all hard angles and sharp edges.

John held a long, bony hand over his head to block the rain. "How are things?" He reached out to put his other hand on Webb's shoulder, but then suddenly pulled it back at the last moment. "What's going on?" His breath reeked of coffee. "Talked to your sister lately?"

"Not lately."

"I saw her last week at the Walmart in Brickerville. Those kids are sure cute."

"Yeah, they are."

"She ever ask about me?" And then he laughed.

Webb wanted to tell John that Shelly was never going to love him. "I haven't talked to her in a while."

"She still married to Harland?"

"Yup."

"He's a good guy."

"Is he?"

John laughed. He looked up and rain got in his eyes. He pressed two long fingers into his sockets and wiped his eyes. "Gosh, I hope so. She deserves a good guy."

"Everyone does."

"That's a good point, Webb," he said. He laughed again. "Well, it's good to see you."

Webb tightened his lips into a smile. "Stay dry, huh."

"You too."

Webb continued walking.

"Hey, if you ever talk to Shelly, tell her I said hello."

Webb walked over to Main Street and climbed the hill. In the gutter he spotted a stray beer bottle. He picked it up. An old woman eyed him with disgust. He wanted to explain that he didn't drink anymore, that he was not the man she knew twenty years ago, stalking the streets, hands clenched in rage. But he said nothing. He stepped aside and let her pass. He threw the bottle into the trash.

27

Alice pushed the key into her lock. A moment later Ruth stuck her head out next door.

"I thought you'd be at work," said Alice.

"Monday's fight night. I don't go on till eleven. Wanna come in?"

"I'm tired. Another time."

Alice shut her door. She turned out the light and climbed into bed fully dressed. She could hear Ruth humming, and she remembered how she used to fall asleep listening to Chick play the piano in the living room. She wondered what he was doing and was suddenly stricken by an impulse to call him. Instead she got up and knocked on Ruth's door.

"Who is it?"

"It's me."

The door swung open. Ruth sat at her table painting her toenails. "The prick cut my pay. His old man used to pay me for the full week but since Ricky took over, he's docking me for fight night. He calls it *prorating*."

Alice took off her shoes and sat on the bed. "What's fight night?"

"They put on these big gloves and go for it right there on the bar floor."

Alice watched her, marveling at her ability to shut out derision. Ruth didn't mention the looks of irritation and quiet disgust she received from the other patrons at Corky's. She seemed oblivious to her pariah status. As they sat in silence, listening to the rain, Alice started to cry.

"What are you doing?"

"Why were you so nice to me?"

"What?" Ruth squirmed uncomfortably.

"I get paid tomorrow, so . . ."

"Hey, I said don't worry about it."

"Maybe I could come with you to work. We could hang out on your breaks."

"That's a no go. I do table dances on my break. That's where I make my tips." Ruth finished her last toe and put the lid back on the bottle. "Sorry sugar. Business comes first."

Alice wiped at her eyes. "I'm afraid I'm not going to be able to sleep."

A car honked outside. Ruth opened the window. "Hold your horses, Ricky, I gotta let my nails dry." The horn honked again. "I'm not putting my goddamn boots on with wet nails," she yelled. Ricky honked his horn in short bursts. "Didn't your daddy teach you nothin'?" Ruth reached into her closet and removed her pumps. She put on her coat, and led Alice into the hall. "Here." She handed her a joint. "This'll help you sleep." She punched Alice on the shoulder. "Take it easy, toots," she said, and she thundered down the hall.

"Hey. Ruth. You're looking good."

"Tell me something I don't know, bee-yotch."

"You wanna get breakfast tomorrow?"

"Give me a holler in the morning," she said, and with a backhanded wave, three hundred pounds of stone fox balanced in size fourteen, scarlet, fuck-me pumps vanished down the stairs.

28

Alice and Ruth sat in the back corner booth of Corky's eating breakfast. "In my dungeon," said Ruth, slathering a thick pat of butter onto her pancake, "I got this steel box where I put my slaves until they behave. That's my ouvre of late, is my dominatrix enterprise. It's more mental than sexual. I'm a student of human nature."

The restaurant was filling up with customers. Alice leaned forward, "Maybe we should just keep it down a little bit," she said.

"Why? Did I say something bad?"

"No, it's just that you don't need everybody knowing your business."

"Honey, haven't you guessed by now, I'm not exactly a private citizen."

Alice noticed Trudy sitting at the counter picking at a muffin like a sparrow. She glanced over at Alice and waved. Alice smiled and waved back.

"So, do you have sex with these people?" Alice whispered.

"Hell, no!" Ruth shoved a forkful of pancake into her mouth. "I remember one time, this Jehovah's Witness gentleman rings my bell, wants to know if he can save me from damnation. I tell him it's too late, but come in for some tea. Inside of five minutes, sweet Howard's down in my basement begging for discipline. So, I put him in the box, then go back upstairs to finish folding my laundry."

While Ruth spoke, Alice noticed Brenda, the lady from Joyce's knitting circle, standing at the front door with her son and her husband, the huge man Ruth took into the alley. Brenda led the way, sitting down at the booth next to Alice and Ruth. She smiled at Alice, but when she saw Ruth her eyes went cold, and she turned away in disgust.

"So I get a call from my next door neighbor that she lost her cat," said Ruth. "Now bear in mind, we're in the suburbs. Her poor little kitty's diabetic, if Billy doesn't get his shots, it's fatal." She lifted a sausage from her plate and sucked it suggestively into her mouth. Alice glanced sideways to see Brenda gripping her menu tightly. She kicked Ruth gently under the table, but Ruth just moved her foot, oblivious. "My neighbors all think I'm a telemarketer. So we go looking for Billy—finally find him sleeping in her closet—but meanwhile I've forgotten there's a little man in a box in my basement. I run back home and sweet Howard is screaming "I surrender, I surrender," which is code for "This ain't fun no more.""

Alice noticed that Brenda was muttering under her breath while studying her menu. She was listening to everything Ruth was saying. "Sickening," she said.

Ruth glanced at the woman. "Excuse me?" she said. "Are you talking to me?"

"Have some decency. We have a child here," said Brenda.

"Really? Which one?" said Ruth. "Only kidding, Doyle,"

she said to the giant man sitting across the table from his wife. Doyle bristled.

Brenda's eyes widened. "You know her?"

Doyle looked at Ruth. "We got our boy here," he said.

Brenda turned to Ruth. "You're useless."

"Least I know how to please a man."

Brenda's face twitched. Alice kicked Ruth under the table. She sensed what Ruth was going to say next, but it was too late. "Ain't that right, Doyle?"

Brenda turned to her husband, trembling with rage. She grabbed her son's hand, pulled him from his seat and dragged him toward the door.

Doyle fixed Ruth with a hard look. "You just fucked up royally." He followed his wife outside. He glanced back and looked at her one more time.

29

Joyce waited for Alice at the door with her arms folded. She led her into the stock room and stared at the floor. "The ladies who come into my shop are respectable people."

"Is this about Ruth?"

"I'm not interested in that thing's name."

"She's my friend," said Alice. "Brenda walked in and started making comments."

"No." A vein pulsed on Joyce's forehead. "No, no, no, no. This is not about Brenda."

Alice stood solidly. "Please don't tell me who to spend time with."

Joyce's pupils wiggled. "I'm not doing this," she said. "No, I refuse it." She unlocked the top drawer of her desk and removed a checkbook. She hurriedly scribbled down a number, signed it, and tore it from the book, then tossed the check on the desk with a snap of her wrist, like she was flicking away a bug.

Alice stared at the check. "This isn't what I want," she said, but when she looked at Joyce, she could see the issue was settled.

* * *

Alice walked through the store, and past Trudy, who stood watching her while biting a fingernail. She pushed open the front door and went outside. She walked down the street to the bank and asked the teller how many days they would hold her check before she could cash it.

"Hold it for what?" he asked.

She walked out of the bank with two hundred and seventy-nine dollars in her purse. Back at the Frontier, she pulled her suitcase from the closet and began filling it with clothes. A moment later there was a knock at the door. She opened it to see Ruth standing in her boxer shorts and a T-shirt that said something clever and untrue about the love lives of truckers.

"I'm leaving," said Alice, throwing her toiletries into a case.

"Where you going?" asked Ruth, chewing on a cord of black licorice.

"Portland. I hate this place."

"What happened?"

"Nothing. I quit."

"Well, I didn't want to say anything, but you don't want to work for that uppity bitch. I knit better'n any one of them ladies."

Alice reached into her purse. "Here." She peeled off two twenties. "I didn't ask for your opinion."

"What's your problem?"

"I told you. Nothing."

Ruth handed the money back. "Here. I said I didn't want it."

"Keep it."

She threw the money on the floor. "What's the matter with

you anyway?"

"Fine. You don't want it, I'll keep it." Alice picked the money off the floor. "You didn't have to say all that stuff at breakfast."

"What? Is that what happened? Did that bitch fire you cause you were hanging out with me?"

"I didn't say that."

"Is that what happened?"

Alice looked into Ruth's eyes. "No. I'm just saying, maybe you don't always have to say everything you're thinking all the time."

"Who the hell are you?" She reached out and pulled the money out of Alice's hand. She folded the bills and tucked them under her bra strap. "Portland ain't cheap, you know."

"I don't care. Anything's better than this place."

"I go there all the time. A place like this'll run you three or four times as much a night."

"I have two hundred and forty dollars," said Alice.

"Did you pay Milo yet?"

"I paid the first night."

"What was that, Tuesday? So, six nights—that's a week, that's one-seventy-five. By the time you buy your gas, that won't cover a night, much less anything to eat."

Alice blinked.

"So whatcha gonna do?"

Alice stared out the window.

Ruth held out a piece of licorice. Alice took it and tore off a bite.

30

A giant fiberglass buffalo loomed over the highway, its front hoof balancing a dinner tray with a burger on top. The sign read: Buffalo Burgers. Alice tried to follow the logic of an animal appearing happy about serving a patty made from one of its own. Behind the restaurant were the remnants of a mini-putt course, a dilapidated windmill and a weather-damaged wooden soldier, all built on various levels with tall weeds springing up from the muddied Astroturf. She walked through the parking lot toward the log cabin structure and pushed open the heavy glass door. A slack-jawed kid with slick black hair glanced up from his mop. His eyes wandered lazily to her chest.

"I'm looking for the manager," she said.

"Back there."

She walked through the kitchen where a couple of men in their mid-twenties chopped vegetables and stacked dishes. "Either one of you the manager?" One of them pointed to a door. She knocked.

A red-haired boy with a forehead rough with pimples

opened the door. "May I help you?"

"I'm looking for the manager."

"That's me." He stuck out his hand. It was cold and limp.

"You're kidding. How old are you?"

"Seventeen."

"I'm Alice."

"Jimmy."

"I heard at the post-office you were looking for help."

"Have you ever waitressed?"

"No, but I'm sure I can figure it out."

"Our waiter died last week, and Dori is struggling to keep up." He led her through to the dining area. "My mother's been helping out, but she has to take care of my sisters."

An older woman pushed open the front door.

"Dori, this is Alice."

She was a sturdy woman with a pleasant face.

"We're talking about maybe her waitressing."

Jimmy walked Alice through the restaurant, a cavernous box filled with photographs of mill workers and lumberjacks. A long bank of golf trophies sat behind a glass case. Heavy booths lined the walls with banquet tables in the center.

"My father bought this place to make it sort of an amusement park, but travelers don't want to stop and play mini-putt, so now he's back at the mill and I quit school to help run things. Where do you live anyway?"

"Right now I'm staying at the Frontier."

"So you take route six? I live on route six. Cliff Shoemaker used to drive me home, but . . ."

"Cliff was your waiter?"

"Did you know him?"

"I cleaned his fridge yesterday," she said. "I could drive you home, if you want."

She went into the bathroom with a couple of Buffalo Burger shirts and pants that she picked off a rack in Jimmy's office. She emerged in a brown and orange Polyester uniform. Jimmy and Dori stood waiting outside the door.

"Does it fit all right?" asked Dori.

"Yeah, why?" They were looking at her strangely. "This wasn't Cliff's uniform, was it?" asked Alice.

"Just the shirt," said Jimmy. "But don't worry, I washed it twice."

"Do you mind me asking? He didn't die in it, did he?"

Jimmy stared at the floor. "I got all the blood out."

"Was there a lot?"

"It was mostly on the collar," said Dori.

"I thought he had a heart attack," said Alice.

"He did," said Jimmy, "but it happened over the fryer." He handed her a badge with her name stenciled at the top above a buffalo with the word TRAINEE written in it. "So people know who you are."

31

Webb was at the cash register ringing up a customer when Lester entered the store. He greeted George, who was prowling the aisles with his ledger. "How's business, old timer?"

"They steal more than they buy." George steadied himself on his cane.

Lester chuckled. "You can't take it with you, buddy."

"You defending that Feeney kid?"

"Yeah. He's a pain in the ass."

"He's a piece of shit, but I don't fault him."

"Let's hope the judge agrees."

"Are you still seeing that girl in Pistol River?"

"Only when I'm bored," said Lester. He stretched his arms and let out a yawn. "I heard your boy here might have a girlfriend."

"Him?"

"She's a fine-looking woman," said Lester. Webb took a cod from the display case to the cutting board. He stuck the knife into the throat before running it carefully through the soft belly to the tail. Lester patted George on the shoulder and sauntered over to the counter.

"How's tricks, Cooley?"

Webb gave Lester a nod.

"Did I hear that right? Heard you had her up to that little room of yours."

Webb held the fish under the tap, letting the guts drain into the sink.

"Must be nice being out, huh?"

Webb placed the cod back on the table and began gently removing the skeleton from the flesh. Lester smiled, eyes half-closed like a cat. Webb faced him, still holding the knife, his fist glistening with blood. "Can I help you with something . . . ?"

A smile flickered across Lester's mouth. "What was it? Twenty years?"

"If not, maybe you should leave." Webb squeezed the knife tightly, his cuticles burning from the fish's scales.

"Is that some kind of threat?" Lester glanced around the room, turning to George and feigning surprise. "Is Webb Cooley threatening me?"

Webb turned back to the table and sliced into another cod, letting the guts drop into the sink while the cold water cleaned its insides. He twisted the tap hard and listened to the water hit the bottom of the steel basin. Lester palmed a packet of gum from the counter and broke it open. With the backsplash, Webb could feel the ocean's spray and the wind drowning out Lester's words, until, through the mist, his words raced toward him, stinging him like a jellyfish.

"Does she know who you are?"

The knife slipped through Webb's fingers and fell into the sink.

"Or have you told her?" Lester popped a stick of gum into his mouth.

Webb looked up, fighting to keep his breath even. "I did my time."

"Yes, you sure did." Lester twisted the gum wrapper between his fingers. "You think that was justice?"

The blood dripped from the tail until there was nothing but a fine pink thread disappearing down the drain. Webb looked at the dead fish in his hands. This was not about justice. It was about a woman. None of them paid attention to the ring of the bell as the front door opened. Webb noticed her first, and from the look in his eye, Lester turned to see her standing at the door. Alice shook the water from her umbrella and placed it in the bin. "Hi there," said Lester, snapping his gum.

"Hi," she said, aware of the tension in the room. She picked up a basket, and walked down the aisle.

Lester looked at Webb, and then at Alice. He tossed the gum wrapper onto the counter and sauntered to the door. He stopped, and Alice glanced back. "Enjoy your evening," he said to her.

"You too."

Lester opened the door and went outside. George looked at Webb. Finally he turned and walked back to the stock room.

"What was that about?" asked Alice.

Webb said nothing. He rang up her purchases. She paid him and he handed her the change. George walked back into the store. "Cooley, I want you to crush up those boxes in the back."

Webb nodded.

"That means now."

Alice looked at George. "He's just finishing with me," she said.

George gazed at her. "I want you back here in one minute, Cooley," he said, before retreating into the stock room.

"Is he having another bad day?"

Webb tried to smile, but he couldn't.

"I got a new job. I'm working at Buffalo Burgers. I was thinking of getting some dinner to celebrate. Do you feel like joining me across the street?"

Webb glanced out the window, as if he might see Lester watching him. "I can't tonight," he said. "I . . ." he started, but trailed off.

"You don't have to explain. I guess I'll see you around."

Webb met her eyes for a moment, and then looked away.

She picked up her umbrella and walked out the door.

32

He sat in his room, staring out the window. He didn't remember six o'clock and turning the sign to read CLOSED. He didn't remember climbing the hill to his apartment, or removing his clothes and taking a shower. But he was here, with a towel around him and an empty plate of food on the table. He didn't remember getting up that morning and putting on his clothes and pouring his cereal, but there was the bowl in the sink, with the handle of the gray spoon peeking out over the edge. He had eaten and worked and come home, but he didn't remember any of it. He stared at the sketches on his walls and wondered about tomorrow, and the next day, and the one after that. He looked at the picture of the slick, black rock that stretched out into the surf, and all he could remember was throwing away the twisted gum wrapper from the counter and placing fifty cents in the till to cover the balance on Lester's gum. He was tired of blocking it all out, of his days bleeding together and vanishing into nothing. He was tired of the stares when he crossed the street.

He put on his boots and went back outside. He ignored the shouts and the laughter coming from the Pastime, and kept his head down as he passed the general store. There was no one at the front desk of the Frontier, so he climbed the stairs. He hesitated before knocking on Alice's door.

"Who is it?"

"It's me," he said. "Webb."

She opened the door and looked at him. "Yes?"

"You asked me where I was going the other day, when I was in my suit. I didn't tell you the truth."

"You mean you weren't going to a meeting?"

He stared at his shoes. "I was going to see my parole officer."

"Oh," she said. "So, you were in prison."

"Yes, ma'am."

The hallway was silent. She turned her head to see if Percy might appear.

"I just wanted to let you know," he said. "Anyway, I'll let you go," he said. He turned and walked down the hall.

She watched him walk away. She didn't want him to leave, but she didn't know if she wanted him to stay.

He stopped and turned. "I'm not the person I used to be." He stood halfway down the hall in his olive sweater under a sickly yellow light. "I can't show you that rock either," he said. "I can't leave the city limits for my first year."

She wanted to tell him it was okay, but she wasn't sure it was, so she said nothing. She just watched as he disappeared down the hall.

33

A lice walked in the surf. The cool wet sand cushioned her
feet.

"Comin' in?" shouted Ruth.

Alice shook her head.

"You gotta come in."

Alice sat on the shore near an anthill, watching Ruth
dancing in the surf in her denim overalls rolled up to the knees.
The waves were choppy and rolling in low for half a mile. The
air was electric. Seagulls flew madly, jostling for food.

"It's frickin' freezing," said Ruth. An ant struggled across
the sand with a speck of straw, dragging it back to the hill. It ran
into a blade of grass and got stuck momentarily until another
ant bumped into it and set it free. A light rain began to fall
making dimples in the sand. Ruth continued dancing in the
surf, twirling and shouting while Alice watched the black line
of ants grow thinner as they disappeared underground.

There was a rumbling, and then a crack as the sky opened
and the rain fell in clumps. Alice shouted over the noise and

Ruth stopped spinning. Alice snatched up their towels. As she ran back to the car, she heard a roar and turned to see Ruth, eyes squeezed, arms outstretched, bellowing at the sky. Seagulls scattered and a pelican that had been sitting on a nearby rock took off low over the water. Alice stood transfixed, and then dropped the towels and sprinted back toward Ruth. Ruth watched as Alice ran into the water up to her shins and began to scream. The two women stood facing each other in the icy water as the rain pelted them. They shrieked at the heavens, but their cries evaporated into the gray clouds.

34

Webb stood down the road watching the men pull into the church parking lot. They greeted each other with handshakes and embraces. He remembered the last time he shook a man's hand. Mr. Hoffman, the Warden, congratulated him on being a model prisoner. He squeezed Webb's hand tight, wished him luck, said he hoped he never saw him again.

He waited for the men to go inside then walked toward the church. He climbed down the stairs and followed the arrow on a small cardboard sign that read Alcoholics Anonymous. A dozen chairs stood in a circle in the middle of the room. He entered and took a seat, avoiding the other men's eyes. They were all speaking to each other. When he looked up, he recognized some faces.

The meeting started. A man shared about the rough time he was having with his wife, how she wanted a baby but he didn't know if they could afford another one. They went around the circle, each man telling something from his life. There was laughter, rowdy, but not unkind. When it was Webb's turn he introduced himself. "My name is Webb. I'm an alcoholic." The men repeated his name. "Hi Webb." And suddenly he couldn't speak. Hearing his name did something to him. It made him angry to feel vulnerable like this. It was like they were taunting him, like they were making him take his clothes off. He tried to speak. "I knew about this meeting, but I was afraid to come," he said. "I haven't had a drink in eight years." He closed his eyes, searching for words. "Some of you know me . . . maybe most of you . . . know what I did. I probably even hurt some of you. If you want me to leave, just say so."

They sat in silence for a moment, and then a man said, "Nobody wants you to leave."

Webb nodded that he was done and the next man began to speak. He could hear Lester's voice: *Do you really think that was justice?* His words grew louder and louder until Webb could not hear anything else. He stood up and walked to the door. They were dangerous, these men, the only thing he shared with them was an allergy to booze. He was afraid of what he would have to confront if he let them into his life. Someone said his name, called him back, but he climbed the steps quickly. It wasn't until he stood outside the church, sucking in cold air, that he was able to register what the man had said. *Webb, it's all right.* But it wasn't, and it never would be.

The cold rain made his hands ache. He zipped up his jacket and walked down the hill to the road.

35

The rain hammered Alice's car. A lone figure with his collar up walked along the side of the road. "Poor son of a bitch," said Ruth.

"I think that's Webb."

"Oooh, I'm in love with him."

Alice slowed down as Webb turned to see the women, bright red and beaming. "Get in!"

He climbed into the back and Alice introduced him to Ruth.

"Sure, I know Webb. He sells me my snacks."

"We're just coming from the beach," said Alice.

Ruth turned around in her seat. "We were thinking of going bowling, would you care to join us?"

The women went back to the hotel to get changed. Webb met them in the lobby with an umbrella. They walked around the corner to Waiden Lanes, a rundown four-lane alley next to an aging Laundromat.

The entrance to Waiden Lanes housed a pair of vintage

pinball machines that blinked and ding, ding, dinged. It smelled like the movie theater lobby back in Seattle where Alice's parents took her on Friday nights. The smell of bleach masked the faint scent of stale popcorn, dirty carpet and damp cedar. An elderly woman watched them approach the counter. Alice noticed the lady nudge her husband.

"God, I hate when people stare," said Ruth.

"Ignore them," said Alice.

"No can do," said Ruth. She glared at the old woman. "Take a picture, lady. It'll last longer."

"Please don't do that," said Alice to Ruth.

They rented shoes from the young man at the counter and were given a lane. Alice took a practice shot while Ruth shoved a fistful of quarters into the jukebox. Lynard Skynard's "Free Bird" came on and Ruth sang along. Her voice rose until she was belting out the words. The old woman muttered something to her husband, and then grabbed her score sheet and together they marched up to the clerk to pay.

While they played, Alice watched Webb. He was quiet. He spoke with economy. "Nice shot, Ruth. You're playing good." He was careful. His movements were graceful. His hands were strong, his fingers thick and well defined.

Alice found herself gazing at his body, his broad shoulders and strong back. He was muscular, but it was a body built from labor. He was like an animal, unselfconscious; it was in the ease with which he lifted the ball from the track. Alice noticed her mind straying. Why did he come to her room to explain his past? He liked her. He wanted her to know him. And here she was, pretending nothing had happened. She told him she was married, and now she was trying to convince herself that they were just bowling. Her mind flashed on her dinner with him— the dizzy warmth she felt when he stood behind her. She'd heard of women who fell for convicts—that distaff subset swooning over incarcerated men, mailing suggestive photos and scented unmentionables as if these men required wooing. She remembered how he looked at her when he fixed her lock, careful, nervous. She wondered what it would be like to be with someone who had not been with a woman for a long time.

"How'd you grow up in a place like this?" Ruth asked. "There's nuthin' to do 'round here 'cept bowlin' or screwin.'"

"Well . . ." Webb's face turned red. "I'd say some did that more than others."

Ruth laughed too loudly. "What the hell does that mean, Webb?"

"I'll leave that up to you," he said.

"I bet you were a stud," said Ruth.

"Ruth," said Alice.

"What?"

"I reckon we were just bored," he said. "Not the most productive way to spend a youth."

At five o'clock, Ruth smacked her hands together and said she had to leave. "Can't miss my six o'clock curtain." She tried to give Alice money for the bowling, but Alice insisted on paying. She watched Ruth march to the front door, elbows stabbing the air.

The bowling alley was empty. She and Webb continued playing, but the sound of the ball hitting pins suddenly seemed too loud. Alice looked at Webb. He asked her if she wanted to stop.

They sat at the snack counter. She had a beer. He ordered water. Sitting next to him, she felt her side growing warm.

A teenage couple entered. They rented shoes, and when they got to their lane they made out on the hard plastic chairs that were bolted to the floor. They leaned against each other, balanced precariously, trying to bridge the distance, their mouths working furiously.

"Those kids are gonna fall," said Webb.

"It'll be worth it."

Alice sipped her beer. She wondered what he had done that put him behind bars. Perhaps it was a case of civil unrest; he turned violent protecting redwoods—or maybe the law simply put away the wrong man. Or he took the rap for a friend. Her mind strayed to darker scenarios, but whatever he had done she didn't want it getting in the way of what was happening now. "I couldn't find the rock," she said.

"It's not easy to find."

She liked the way he measured his words, the way his eyes searched for images when he spoke. He talked with precision, as though something was at stake. She found herself studying his face for clues.

"I was afraid I scared you off," he said.

She shook her head. The young couple left. The clerk told them he was closing. Alice reached for her purse, but Webb stopped her and placed five dollars on the counter. She thanked him and they walked to the door. He opened his umbrella and held it over her as they walked together in the rain.

She stopped outside the hotel. "If you're still around in February I can show you that rock," he said.

She smiled. "I'm afraid I probably won't be here then."

"I figured."

He turned away. She ducked into the narrow alcove. She was about to open the front door, then stopped and peeked out to watch him climb the hill. His shoulders were slightly rounded. His hands moved stiffly at his sides. There was something courageous in his gait. She wondered if what he had done was forgivable.

36

She tried to sleep, but her mind played tricks. She wondered if Chick was right, if this was an escape. Chick was smart. He saw things she couldn't see, and presented himself with utter assurance which left her feeling unsure of everything. If marrying him was a mistake, and she was fairly sure that it was, then she chastised herself for staying so long, which only led her to rationalize why it was *not* a mistake, so she could return to him and not have to deal with the shame of denial. But what if she returned, only to discover later, in some definitive way, that it was a mistake? How could she live with herself? She rolled over and tried to dodge the mattress spring that seemed to follow her around the bed. She wondered how long it would be before she kicked her dependency on Chick and trusted herself not to go back. A week? A year? Would she be here in February for Webb to show her the rock? The thought made her wince. What would it take to find something in herself, a rudder to steer herself out of this place? She replayed her night and wondered if these were her people, an ex-con and a stripper. As her brain fought sleep, it wandered, it asked open-ended questions like how does one measure the quality of a human being? In her mind, she listed what she valued: integrity, honesty, kindness, compassion—and then she thought about Chick. The truth, she had to admit, was that her highest values were creative achievement, public acclaim, and financial success, and if she was truly honest, she could probably institute a point system to determine compatibility with perhaps a couple of bonus points left over to cover the more ephemeral qualities like graciousness and tact. But, was that a bad thing? Was it not human nature to be drawn to achievement? Surely creative success was an indicator of secondary traits like perseverance, passion, emotional intelligence, and a poetic spirit. But what about those who possessed great wisdom but didn't play an instrument? Did they score a zero? Were they completely off her radar? Was creativity limited to the arts, or was it also a way of seeing the world? Alice felt a clawing in her belly. It was an alien thought she did not want to follow to its conclusion because she did not anticipate that leaving Chick might mean she would have to change. What if she was incapable? But if she didn't understand what drove her to him, how could she be sure she wouldn't repeat it? She saw it all the time; folks left their spouses only to do the dance with someone else.

Her brain was tired, but she couldn't shut it off. She wanted a solution. Her mind kept circling back to Chick.

Why *did* she leave him? Was it fair to blame him for her inability to paint? And if that was a bullshit reason, how else was she kidding herself? Was leaving him another bullshit reason? Did she expect too much? She was suddenly struck by the notion that her leaving had nothing to do with him, that she could spend the rest of her days running from him, but until she committed to something, she might never run toward

anything. If she couldn't change, then she was stuck, forever
prey to any man who offered her the promise of a glamorous
life. There was an unspoken agreement, a tacit understanding
that if she built her own life separate from him the marriage
would end. A negotiation had taken place, and although it was
silent, it was clear that she offered him her youth in exchange for
security—but more than that, and this was the part she didn't
foresee: she must remain young, a girl, with few opinions, little
ambition, and only friends of his choosing. She must dedicate
her life to him, to his worldview, and in exchange, their life
together would be fabulous.

She sat up in bed, wide awake, her blood hammering
under her skin. She turned on the light and stared at the frayed
curtains. Her palms sweated. Something needed to change.
Now. Now. She couldn't take it for one more minute. Her brain
screamed. Yet she had to remain steadfast in her decision to
stay away from Chick. But what if steadfastness was a mask
for inflexibility? Was she holding onto some old idea that
no longer served her? What if she wasted more time doing
something else that didn't work? What if she spent the rest of
her life chasing one idea after another that led nowhere? She
knew what she wanted. She wanted to paint. So, why did she
quit? Was it because of Chick's frog comment? Really? She
could have continued painting, even if he didn't support her,
but it was easier to blame him than it was to take the risk. So,
if that was true, then why did she leave him? It wasn't until she
held her cell phone to her ear and listened to its ring that she
realized she had gone into her closet, dug the phone from her
suitcase and dialed his number.

When she heard his voicemail message, her lungs seized.
He spoke in the dry, slightly robotic tone of a telephone
operator. "Hi there. Leave a message. If this is an emergency,

hang up and dial 911."

She was smiling when she heard the beep. She was about to hang up when a call came through. She answered it.

"Hello?" she said.

"Who's this?"

She listened to his voice, listened for the anguish, the rawness of sleepless nights.

"It's Alice."

"Where are you?"

"Oregon."

"What are you doing there?"

"I'm living here."

He sniffed. She could tell he was high. She wondered how much he had drunk.

"Can we talk?"

"I can't talk right now," he said.

"Why not?"

"Look, Alice. I gave you a good life. I don't know what else to tell you."

"I just want to talk."

"I don't have anything to say." He sighed. "If you want to talk, go ahead."

"Why does that make me feel guilty? Why do I feel bad for wanting to hear your voice?"

"Let's do this in the morning," he said.

"Fine," she said. And then she heard something. She wasn't sure if it was a sound, a rustling, or just her intuition, but she sensed that somebody else was there.

"You're not alone, are you?"

"I'll talk to you tomorrow."

"Don't hang up."

"Here we go."

"Who is it?"

"I'm hanging up."

"I don't care who it is. It doesn't matter."

She didn't hang up the phone. She hurled it, and let the wall do it for her. Even as she threw it, she knew it was not an act of rage, but of self-preservation, a precautionary measure. She needed something to prevent her from calling him back. There was power in believing he wanted her back, that he couldn't live without her, that her absence made a difference. But she was not prepared for this.

37

She knocked on Ruth's door, but there was no answer.

She went down to the lobby, measuring her breath. A couple of mill workers sat on the couch sharing a flask. One of them said something to her, but she couldn't hear it. She hurried outside and stood at the curb, knowing there was only a short time before it all came crashing down. She couldn't breathe. Her brain filled with noise. She crossed the street to the Pastime and pushed open the door. It was larger than she expected, long and narrow with rows of old tables that had names whittled into the wood, crude tokens of lost loves. A pool table sat at the rear underneath a large Confederate flag mirror. She saw Lester at the bar talking with two other men. One of them nudged him, but before he had time to see her, she turned and slipped back outside.

She stood under the awning for a moment before starting across the street.

"Hey!"

She turned to see Lester jogging toward her.

"Where you going?" His boots clacked on the pavement. "Let me buy you a drink."

"Thanks, I can't."

He had a strange expression. "What happened?"

"I, I . . ." she laughed. "My husband's . . ." she couldn't finish the sentence. She could feel the tears coming.

"I thought you left him?"

"I did. I did leave him. I didn't know it was gonna be permanent. You don't understand women, Lester. I know you think you do."

"Whoah." He stepped back. "I just asked if I could buy you a drink."

She put her hands to her face. "I'm sorry. I'm upset right now."

"Come on in and have a drink. You're gonna be okay."

"No," she said. "I can't. Too many people."

"We'll go back to my place."

She smiled painfully. "No, I think I'm just gonna go back to my room."

"You sure?"

"Yeah, I better go."

He nodded. "Okay. Suit yourself."

She walked toward the Frontier Hotel. She looked back and watched Webb go inside his apartment building, and then she began walking up the hill.

"I thought you were going back to your room."

Lester stood under the awning watching her.

She stopped. "Do I owe you something?"

She waited for him to respond, but he stood there, dumbstruck. She continued climbing the hill.

"You know who he is, don't you? I mean, you do know what he did."

"Yes, Lester, I do. I know what he did. And if we were all judged by our pasts, I don't imagine any of us'd fair too well."

He cocked his head.

She held his look. "And wipe that grin off your face. Has he bothered you or anyone since he was paroled?"

Lester scratched his nose. "Nope."

"Then stop pretending you're trying to help me out."

Lester nodded. He walked back into the bar.

38

She knocked on Webb's door. There was a rustling, the sound of bedsprings, and then the light blinked on under the doorway.

"Who is it?"

She hesitated. She wanted to run. Thoughts stormed through her brain. Is this a mistake? Is it over with Chick? Am I doing this for revenge? She wondered if she could go back to her room and endure the pain. "It's me. Alice."

The door opened. He stood there in a white T-shirt and boxer shorts. "Are you okay?"

She pressed herself into him.

The room was quiet, except for the rumble of a car and the sound of tires on the wet street.

She kissed him on the mouth and he kissed her back.

They stood at the end of his bed. She was watching it all from far away. Chick's breath always tasted like weed. Webb's mouth tasted clean, faintly of mint.

She ran her fingers over him, feeling the hard muscles

under his skin. She wanted to escape the noise in her head. She closed her eyes and let him touch her.

"Please turn out the light," she whispered.

She lay back on the bed. The room went dark.

She remembered standing in this room just a few nights earlier, staring at his bed, imagining herself in it.

He ran his fingers down her back. She felt the strap pull away from her skin, and then the click as he unsnapped her bra. She tried to make a joke. "They haven't changed," she said. He was silent.

"You're beautiful," he said.

"Is it okay that I'm here?" she asked. But she wasn't asking him. She was talking to herself.

He cupped her breasts and kissed her neck. He ran his hand down to the curve of her waist.

She lay down on her back. The sheets were warm. The faintest light came in through the window.

She moved against him, slowly at first, her hips rising rhythmically. Her nearness awakened something in him. The tight rage inside began to loosen. She hooked her thumbs into her jeans and pulled them off. He was on his knees on the mattress. He pulled off his shirt.

She opened her legs. She reached down between his legs and felt him stiffen. She touched him, her fingers gently running up and down him. He moved on top of her. She gripped his shoulders as he slid inside.

She gasped. "Yes," she said. "Yes. Yes. Yes."

39

Jimmy paced the kitchen.

Alice entered. "What's wrong?"

"Alice." He looked terrified. "I need your help."

She followed him out to one of the booths.

"This is Bethany." He pointed to a big-boned blonde girl who sat squeezed between two other girls. "And this is Laura and Jane." He was smiling and trying to act casual, but his voice trembled. "Ladies," he said, "this is Alice, our finest waitress."

The girls giggled.

"Alice, would you please take good care of them?"

"Of course I will," she said.

When she returned to the kitchen Jimmy passed her with a tray of Arnold Palmers. "These are on the house," he said, his eyes fixed on the floor in case he tripped.

Later, he approached her, his forehead coated in sweat. "I'm getting this," he said, taking the bill from her tray. "And this is for you," he said, handing her a ten-dollar bill.

"Jimmy, no."

"Take it."

"You can't give me ten dollars."

"Please."

"I'm not taking it. Now stop it."

"Okay. Well, I owe you," he said.

40

Webb walked into the dark interior of the U.S. Post Office and Secondhand Treasures. He squinted, his eyes adjusting to the light. The room was a cloud of smoke and smelled of patchouli incense. "Mitzi? You back there?"

"Webb? Is that you?" said Mitzi, looking up from her magazine.

Webb approached. "Hey," he said.

Mitzi lit a cigarette. "You need some stamps?"

"No."

"What can I help you with?"

"I'm looking for a kitchen table." His eyes scanned the room. "And a coupla chairs."

"How big? We got a two-top in the corner." She pointed to a Formica table with chrome legs.

He stepped around a cat. He pushed on the table with a finger. It wobbled a little. "Any others?"

"That's it." She sucked on her cigarette. "You can have it for fifteen. One of those legs is kinda wonky, but you can prop it up." He removed his wallet and counted out the money. He placed the cash on the counter. "How you doin'?" she asked.

He dropped his eyes and stared at the counter, pretending to misunderstand her tone for something more casual. He waited for her to count it before going back to the table. He picked it up and put it over his head. He carried it to the door.

"I'll come back for the chairs," he said.

"Any problem with it, you can return it," said Mitzi. "No questions."

The door closed behind him and she went back to her magazine.

41

A lice pulled out of the parking lot of Buffalo Burgers with Jimmy in her passenger seat. Jimmy kicked off a shoe and stuck his foot on the dashboard. He gazed out the window at the tree line. "Aren't these trees something?" he said.

"They sure are," said Alice.

"You don't see colors like this anywhere else in the world." Jimmy balanced the steel box on his lap that held the day's receipts. A pair of cottontail rabbits bounced across the road in front of them. Jimmy took aim with his pointer finger and snapped his bubblegum through a gap in his front teeth. "Really stunning colors," he said.

"They seemed like nice girls," said Alice.

"You mean Bethany and them?"

"Yeah."

"Yeah, they're nice."

"Is she your girlfriend?"

"Bethany?"

Alice smiled. Jimmy liked saying her name.

"Yeah, I guess so. I'm taking her to the Halloween dance."

"That should be fun."

Alice sped down the county line past the handmade sign that read MISTY'S ONE MILE.

"So, you were married, huh?"

"Still am," she said.

"But it's over?"

She looked at him. "I think so."

"Can I ask you something?"

"Sure."

"Well . . ." He cleared his throat. "We sort of did it the other night, and it was kind of like, one of my first times." He spotted a rabbit out the window. He took aim and blew another bubble. "I heard some guys talking about being *good in bed*. And I was just wondering . . . ?"

"What it means?"

"Yeah."

"I think it just means you want to make the other person feel good."

"Right," he said. His eyes scanned the side of the road for another rabbit. "And that's it?"

"Well," she said. "And taking your time. Sometimes it takes longer for girls to get where they need to go."

"Like, say, how long?"

"It depends on the girl. You know. As long as it takes."

"As long as what takes?"

"You know," she said, and then she waited, hoping to not have to finish the sentence. But Jimmy was silent. A rabbit hopped through the field, but this time he let it live. "For her to have an orgasm," she said. They both watched the rabbit disappear into the tree line. "It's one of those things that's fun to practice," she said.

"I guess," he said, and snapped his gum.

42

A lice and Webb sat at the food counter of Waiden Lanes. She pressed her cheek against his face. His hand dropped to her behind and she moved it away. When he returned it, something shifted inside her and she began to laugh. Her eyes burned and she laughed harder. She could feel herself moving away, floating out of her body. "What is happening," she said. Every time she looked at Webb, she lost control. Another wave exploded.

Two smooth-faced boys stood at the counter. "She's losin' it," said one of them.

"I am," she said. "I am losing it."

Webb put his hand on her lower back. Her body flinched and she fell into another fit of strangled laughter.

"I can't breathe. What is happening to me?" Webb looked at her, puzzled.

"I have to go to the bathroom."

* * *

Webb watched her walk to the other end of the bowling alley, near the entrance. She disappeared into the restroom, and a moment later an old woman emerged. The woman looked at him, then looked away quickly. He wondered what she knew. He wondered if she had said anything to Alice. The woman walked back to her lane, picked up a ball and rolled it down the center for a strike. Her husband marked her score. Then he grabbed a ball, danced to the lane and flung it into the gutter. The old lady barked, "Your legs is too stiff."

He snapped his fingers.

*   *   *

Alice stood in the bathroom and took deep breaths. She splashed cold water on her face. She started to cry. "Oh God, I'm a mess," she said. She thought about her mother and father, and knew they were wondering where she was. This was unfair to them, but she needed to be alone, or at least, away from everything she knew, everything that was familiar. "What am I doing?" she asked herself. She felt giddy and terrified, like she was floating outside of her body, watching it all from a corner of the ceiling. This can't last, she told herself. You should not be doing this.

She pushed on the door and walked back to the counter. "Sorry," she said.

"Are you okay?"

"I don't know," she said. "Maybe we should go."

Outside the air was cold and still. He hooked his arm into hers and a current went through her. They walked slowly back to The Frontier. They stood out front and he asked her if she wanted to come up to his room. Three men stood under the Pastime awning smoking cigarettes. The men stopped talking when Alice and Webb began climbing the hill. She heard one of them mutter something. She couldn't make out the words, but when Webb dropped his arm from around her waist she knew it was about them.

She removed her raincoat and placed it over the tub in his bathroom. The kitchen table and chairs stood between his bed and kitchenette. "I got it on my lunch break," he told her.

She turned out the light and went to him. When they kissed he reached up and unsnapped her bra. He lifted her to the narrow bed and lay next to her. They kissed deep and hard. She moved her pelvic bone against his hand. She lay under him, and as they made love, she felt herself fall away.

Afterwards, she studied herself in his bathroom mirror, cheeks flushed, lips full, and she saw what she had looked like before she got married. It wasn't youthfulness, it was something else, a softness, an unguarded quality around her eyes that surprised her because she hadn't realized that it was gone.

She climbed back into bed and touched the scar on his forearm. Running her finger along its glassy surface she asked, "What happened?"

He stiffened. He shook his head, and they sat quietly until the moment passed.

They sat naked at the table.

He cut a pear into slices and they ate them from a plate with figs.

"Where did you get the figs?"

"George has them delivered from Portland."

"They're really good," she said. "And I see you got a new table."

"I got it next door at Secondhand Treasures."

"I hope it wasn't too much."

"No. I needed to get one."

"Maybe I should pay for half of it."

He stared at his hands. "Why?"

"I don't know. Since I'm sharing it with you."

He glanced outside, down at the Pastime.

"I just don't want you doing it for *me*," she said.

He scratched a rough patch of residual packing tape off the table's surface. "What if I said I'd been planning to get one?"

"Were you?"

He stared at her blankly. "Why didn't you sleep here last night?"

"Because I'm married." She went to the bed and began getting dressed. "I just want to be clear about what this is."

"What is it?"

"I don't want to get serious," she said.

She could hear men shouting outside and she wondered if it was safe to walk back to her room by herself.

"I'm sorry," she said. She grazed his arm as she walked past him. She straightened her shirt. "Maybe this was a mistake."

43

Alice dropped Jimmy off at his house after work and drove back to the hotel.

She climbed the stairs and walked down the hall to her room. She locked the door behind her. She stared at the bed she'd made that morning with the three cigarette burns at the top of the sheet. She'd been dreading this moment, hoping all day that something would happen to prevent her from confronting the night alone. Alone with her thoughts, her mind kept straying to Chick and to what he was doing, and to who he was with. A part of her still clung to the hope that if everything went south she could return to him, and now she wondered if that was still possible. She imagined him having sex with this other woman and she felt queasy, but it was the sudden image of this woman making him laugh that made her recoil. Alice could never make him laugh, only smirk. When she imagined Chick laughing with this other woman her brain spat out scenarios of the two lovers locked in intense gazes, sharing private jokes, feeding each other osso buco while reading passages from *Tropic of Cancer* by candlelight. She wondered who this mystery girl was that amused him, that didn't lose herself in his presence, that navigated his moods. Who was this girl that *got him*? And did he *get her*? Alice went numb at the thought that Chick might have found someone he liked. She imagined this fantasy woman, luscious, sophisticated, daring, and blithely unafraid of him— vulnerable and impenetrable, Chick's perfect lady, his soul mate who provided him with everything that Alice lacked.

She stood over the garbage pail and stared at the remains of her phone, its stray wires and glass shards scattered at the bottom of the can. She thought about Webb and their conversation the night before, and she didn't understand why she'd said it was a mistake.

She had to get out of her room. She could go to a restaurant. There was a pizza place at the top of the hill, but it looked more like a take-out joint. There was a barbecue place a block over, but it sat next to Joyce's store, and she didn't want to go anywhere near there. She could go across the street to Corky's and read a book. She could go for a walk. She could go to the Pastime and have a drink, but she didn't want to risk running into Lester, especially not after their last exchange. Besides, he might tell her about Webb, and she wasn't sure she wanted to hear it. Or maybe she did. Maybe that would prevent her from going back to him. What if she went across the street and asked him what Webb did that put him in prison? She wouldn't even have to ask. She could let him tell her and act like she already knew.

She put on her jacket. She walked down the hall and downstairs. She walked through the lobby, and outside, and began climbing the hill. As she walked, she noticed that she was not crossing the street to the Pastime. She told herself to cross the goddamn street. Why are you not crossing the street? With each step she moved closer to Webb's apartment. Why are you doing this? You cannot do this. Stop. Turn around. Put some distance between yourself and Webb. Do it now before you go any further. But she didn't want to know. What if Lester told her something that prevented her from seeing Webb? She suddenly realized that she needed Webb to keep her from going back home.

She pushed open the heavy door and climbed the stairs. She knocked on his door.

He looked at her, unblinking, but said nothing.

"I don't know what this is," she said.

He put on his jacket. He took her hand and they walked outside.

The sky was black. Thick drops fell from the oak trees that lined the road at the top of the hill. They walked past the small stone church. His arm fell across her shoulder and she wrapped hers around his waist.

"I used to go to church every Sunday when I was a kid," she said. "It seems silly how a sensible person can believe in God."

"Maybe they don't have a choice," he said.

"We all have a choice," she said.

A car approached from behind them. They stepped to the side of the road. As the car passed, a woman, a few years younger than Alice, looked at her and Alice caught her expression. Alice squirmed. Webb's arm fell from her shoulder.

They walked back to his room without speaking. He took off his coat. He went to the fridge and removed a pitcher of water. He poured them each a glass. She sat at the table, still in her coat. "Do you pray?"

He nodded.

"What do you pray for?"

"Nothing." He shrugged. "I just talk to Him," he said. "Say what I need to say."

"Like what?"

"Like, thank you. Or I tell Him what I'm in fear about. Sometimes I just curse Him."

"You can do that?"

"Not all the time. I usually apologize later."

She lifted her glass and toasted him. "Maybe I'll pray to the son of a bitch." She sipped her water.

She stood up. She walked to the door. "Where are you going?" he asked.

"Back to my room."

"Stay here tonight."

"I can't," she said.

"Because you're married? Is that really why?"

"I don't think you should have anything to do with me. I don't think this is fair to either of us. But I don't want to go." She wanted to ask him what he was in prison for, but she didn't want another reason to leave.

He put his arms around her and pulled her tightly into him. He kissed her. He took her hand and led her to the bed. "I can't," she whispered, but she didn't resist. She pulled her sweater over her head. "Somehow I don't think this is going to end well."

The heater sputtered. Cars rolled past outside. She held him tightly. "I'm sorry," she whispered.

"Do you want to stop?"

"No."

She dug her fingernails into his back. When she came her whole body shook.

Afterwards, they lay in bed. "What is it like for you?" she asked. "Making love?"

He stared at the ceiling. "It's been a long time," he said. "I want to be careful."

She ran her hand slowly down the side of his naked body. "I don't want you to be careful," she said.

*   *   *

After that, the wolf came out. He fucked her hungrily, their bodies slick with sweat. She would finish work each day, drop Jimmy off at his house and then drive to the Frontier where she parked her car and walked the few steps up the hill to Webb's building. He would open the door and pull her into him. They barely spoke. They tore off their clothes and climbed into bed where they went at each other like they were trying to rid themselves of their pasts.

One night, after making love, she lay under the sheets, and watched Webb walk to the bathroom. Steam rose off his shoulders.

44

One Saturday the sky cracked open and rain fell like a snare drum on her car roof. Her wipers swung hard. She parked outside Webb's apartment and ran to his front door.

She lay next to him in the darkness moving further away from her past. For years she convinced herself that sex with Chick had been *incredible* but now she wondered how much of it had been a performance. Sex with Webb was different. She came all the time.

Alice and Webb sat in a booth at Corky's watching the water spill over the curb and flow in a small river down the hill.

"How much water can the sky hold?" she asked.

She recognized many faces in the restaurant. She avoided their eyes. She smiled at them from a distance. She had a secret. Her secret was that she did not know what they assumed she did. She studied their faces for signs of who Webb might be.

They sat at the table eating dinner. "We're just having sex," she said.

"You keep saying that."

"I don't want anyone getting hurt."

He looked out the window. "It's too late for that," he said.

A man opened the door. He stomped his feet on the mat. He carried no umbrella, his coat was torn and his work pants soaked through to the skin. Old and thin, with hard lines across his forehead, his eyes bugged when he grinned at the waitress. He sat at the counter, removed a menu from the metal clip, and buried his face in it.

"Phyllis. Gimme some liver and a Michelob."

"How 'bout saying please, Gus?"

The man spoke to himself in a mechanical drone like an engine that wouldn't quit. His mouth moved silently as his eyes jerked from one person to the next. When he saw Alice, his eyes gleamed. He winked. She turned away, but when she glanced back, he was still staring. His eyes danced madly, like he was the life of some party that didn't exist. When Webb turned to see what she was looking at, he spun his head back to her.

"My, my," said the man.

Webb signaled to the waitress for the bill.

"Bring it, bring it," muttered the man, snapping his fingers, his eyes fixed on Webb.

"Who *is* that?" asked Alice.

"What's wrong, can't ya speak?" said the man to Webb. He laughed a high, asthmatic laugh. "You're looking at me," he said to Alice.

Alice turned away.

"Gus, that's enough," said Phyllis, placing the bill in front of Webb.

"That's enough," said Gus. A wet fart trilled from his trousers.

"Let's go." Webb removed his wallet and paid the bill. They walked to the door. Gus was hunched over his food, picking at his French fries like an animal.

She took Webb's hand and they walked in the rain.

"Who was that?"

Webb walked stiffly, staring straight ahead. "That was my father."

They entered his apartment. He went to the window and stared down at the street. She stood in the doorway. "What happened?"

"To *him*?" he said, knowing that was not what she meant. But she saw his fear and nodded. "He's sick," said Webb, like there was no more to say, as if to say more would complicate what he had spent a lifetime trying to simplify.

"When did you see him last?"

"I don't want to talk about this."

"Okay."

She boiled some water for tea.

"Twenty years," he said.

"Is that how long you were in prison?"

He nodded. "Are you gonna take your coat off?"

She removed her coat and draped it over the tub. Her voice wavered, "Are you going to speak to him?"

"I just did."

She sat down at the table across from him. "Did he ever go to prison?"

"No. Just me." He squeezed his eyes shut. "He wasn't a father to my sister. He did things a father shouldn't do." His face turned away. "I didn't want to believe what was going on. And now she's living up the road with a husband that's no good. And there's nothing I can do about it."

"It's not your fault."

"I should have done something."

"You didn't know."

He looked pained. "I did," he said. "At the end I knew."

"The end?" she asked.

He watched her carefully, studying her eyes.

"What happened?" she asked.

"Things got out of control," he said, and he left it there, as if he had answered her question. "The reason I can't leave the city limits . . . when I gave my statement to the police, I said I was going to kill him. Now I have to stay a hundred feet from him for the first year."

"*You* can't go near *him?*" she asked. "Did your sister ever visit you?"

Webb's head moved slightly to the side, as if he was willing memories to be shoved aside or rearranged. "Twice."

"In twenty years?"

"She was too young when I went in. Couldn't drive. By the time she could go, she already had her first kid and was mixed up with some guy, didn't want her to do nothing with me."

She took his hand and interlaced her fingers with his. She studied his fingers, the blanched tips and pinpoint blisters. "What happened?"

He explained how George required him to distribute the ice without gloves.

"Why don't you say something?" she asked.

"No," he said.

"What are you afraid of? You can get another job."

"No. I can't."

She went to the sink for more tea. She poured it, but then she set it down and went to the bathroom for her coat.

"I want you to stay tonight."

She stood at the door. It happened fast, but he saw it in her eyes, a flash of terror. "I want you to see a doctor about your hands," she said.

45

He lay on his bed, and then got up and walked outside into the night.

At the bottom of the hill, he shoved two quarters into the payphone and dialed his sister's number. He stared across the road at the streetlights dotting the river. A man's voice answered.

"Harland?"

"Who's this?"

"It's Webb. My sister there?"

Harland didn't speak.

"Hello?"

"We had your old man over the other day. Too bad you couldn't join us, huh?"

Webb said nothing.

"What's the matter, can't speak?"

"How you doing, Harland?"

"Pfft." There was a long silence. He could hear movements on the other end of the line, and then Harland saying something to Shelly.

After a while, his sister came to the phone. "Webb?"

"Is it okay I called?"

"What do you mean?"

"How are you doing?"

"I was just putting the kids down. It was Tommy's birthday last week." She sounded tired. "He's seven. Brandy's gonna be nine in November."

"My God." Webb forced a chuckle. He could hear Harland telling her to get off the phone.

"I'll just be a minute," she said. "Webb, I gotta go."

"Hey."

"What?"

She already sounded far away.

"I just wanted to say, you know, when you were younger, and all that stuff that happened with Dad . . ."

"Webb, I gotta go."

"I just . . . I shoulda done more. I always wanted to tell you that."

"Anyway."

"You know what I mean."

"I know, Webb." There was a long silence. He wondered if she was crying. Harland yelled something from another room. "Webb, I gotta go."

"I love you, Shelly."

"Bye."

* * *

He walked back up the hill breathing in the cold air. Corky's was empty now. The waitress slouched in a booth counting her receipts while the cook nursed a beer across from her. Webb held his umbrella over his head and watched the thick layer of water roll over the tips of his shoes.

It was during his second week of freedom that he went for lunch with Shelly. He met his niece and nephew for the first time. Harland ate meatloaf in silence, except when he scolded the children for eating with their fingers. There was violence in his voice. Afterward, they planned to go for a walk up the river, but Shelly made an excuse about the kids needing a nap. They promised to stay in touch. For months Webb dreamt about what he would do if he was left alone with Harland, but lately, the dreams subsided and when he thought about him now he just felt an ache.

46

Mitzi sat behind the counter watching TV. She looked up to see Alice and Ruth standing in front of her. Ruth held a moldering sheet of plastic. "This used to be a shower curtain."

Milo emerged from the back office stirring a cup of coffee with a straw.

"They want a new shower curtain," said Mitzi.

Milo stared at the sheet and scratched his beard.

"Bring him a receipt and he'll reimburse you," said Mitzi.

Ruth and Alice grinned.

*   *   *

The Frontier's laundry room was a damp cement basement with exposed pipe running low across the ceiling. The room smelled of fabric softener and wet magazines. Alice and Ruth sat together listening to the lazy rumble of dryers and the rhythmic click of metal.

"How's it going with Webb?" asked Ruth. "I hardly see you lately."

"It feels like something is happening," said Alice. "I wasn't expecting this. I thought I was just going to have a little fun, but I like him."

Ruth tilted her head back and laughed. Her eyes disappeared into fleshy folds.

"What's so funny?" asked Alice.

"You're his girlfriend."

47

A lice sat in the waiting room of the Waiden Health Center, a large renovated brick house at the top of the hill. A nurse sat at the front desk pretending to type while studying her through the glass. Alice waited for twenty minutes, flipping through a magazine, and then the thin wood door opened and Webb appeared.

"What did the doctor say?"

"Nothing serious. Some nerve damage on the fingertips," he said. "A little arthritis in the hands." He glanced at the nurse and she turned away. "C'mon."

They walked outside. He held the umbrella over them and pulled her close.

"Did you know that nurse back there?"

"Yeah, from high school."

"Why didn't she say hello?"

He shrugged. "I reckon most of these folks don't know what to make of me."

"What else did the doctor say?"

"I should probably start wearing gloves."

"Probably? You're going to wear them from now on, aren't you?"

"I don't know."

"What do you mean?" she said.

He pulled away from her.

"Why can't you just tell George that that's what you're going to do?" she said.

He stopped walking and she stepped into the rain. "You want to know why?" he said.

The way he said it scared her. She stepped back. She didn't want to know, but still she asked, "Why?"

"Because I have nowhere else to go," he said. "Nobody else will hire me."

"Can we go?" she said. "I'm getting wet."

He didn't move. He handed her the umbrella.

"You're getting soaked," she said. She tried to cover him with the umbrella but he stepped away. "If you don't want to see me anymore . . ." She didn't finish her sentence.

"Don't do that," he said.

"What?"

"Threaten me."

"I told you not to expect anything from me," she said, and then added, "We're just getting to know each other."

"Is that what we're doing?" He took her wrist. "So, what is it you want to know?"

"Let me go."

"Do you want to know why I was in prison?"

She stared at him, terrified. "Let me go."

"Why don't you ask me why I was in prison?"

A light went on in a room above them. He let her go.

"Don't ever do that again," she said. She threw his umbrella onto the sidewalk and walked back toward the hotel.

He stood in the rain for a few minutes, then picked up the umbrella. The light went off in the room above him, but he could see the silhouette of a figure staring down at him. He walked back to his room.

An hour later there was a knock at his door.

"Who is it?" he asked.

"It's me," said Alice.

She had changed into a pair of dark jeans and a rust-colored sweater. Her hair smelled of shampoo.

"You said you're not that person anymore," she said. "I believe you."

He held the door and let her inside.

"I want to know who you are," she said. "I'm just not ready yet."

They lay together, their skin warm against each other. She fell asleep and he held her, listening to her breath.

She woke up with a start.

"It's okay," he said.

She squeezed him tightly until she fell back to sleep.

48

Webb laced his shoes. His chair moved against the wooden floor and Alice sat up in bed. She wiped her eyes.

"What was it like in prison?" she asked.

He stared at the floor.

"You think you'll go crazy, but you don't," he said. "You just shut down. Make yourself fit into this little square. When you come out, you're not different. You're just smaller."

She said nothing. Just listened. She wanted to tell him she understood, but how could she?

"Everyone knows me here," he said. He wanted to say more, but he stopped. She knew what he meant. She saw how people looked at him, at both of them. She liked it at first, because she liked to cause trouble. Her father used to say she made her life more difficult than it needed to be. She thought it was a compliment. But now she understood what he meant.

Webb walked over and kissed her forehead. "You stayed the night."

"I guess I did."

"I'll be back."

"I'll be gone," she said. "But I'll see you tonight."

He went outside.

*   *   *

Jane Tripp signed her name at the bottom of Webb's file and slid it back across her desk to him. "Is there anything else, Mr. Cooley?"

Webb looked at the narrow mesh-wire window that ran across the length of her office. "I've been spreading the ice with my hands." He showed her the black dots on his fingertips. "Doctor says I got arthritis, but George doesn't want me wearing gloves."

"Why not?"

"Says they contaminate the fish."

The dog yawned at Tripp's feet.

"Would you like me to talk to him?"

"It won't change anything."

"That doesn't sound like a very positive attitude."

"I want another job."

"We've gone over this, Mr. Cooley."

"He'll fire me if I use 'em. He'll find a reason."

"Is that what he said?" She wrote something down in her file.

Webb shifted in his chair.

"I think you need to let people do their jobs, Mr. Cooley."

"My name's Webb."

"All right, I think we're done for today. Please hand your file back to the receptionist."

Webb stood slowly. The dog followed him with his eyes as

he took his file from the desk and walked to the door.

John sat in his police car at the curb when Webb walked through the parking lot. He climbed out and jogged up to Webb.

"Looks like Ned's in some deep trouble with those Mexicans. He told Lester he was thinking of maybe defending himself."

"Ned should be grateful to have a good lawyer," said Webb.

John asked him a question about his sister, but Webb couldn't hear him.

"I better head back," said John.

Webb nodded and kept walking.

49

Webb was sweeping the floor of the General Store when he heard the truck horn. He rested the broom against the counter and stepped into the alley. George emerged from the truck and hobbled to the rear. He didn't say a word as Webb pulled on the rusty chrome handle and opened the back door. He carried the fish into the store, and when he emptied the bags of ice into the display case he returned to the stock room for the gloves that he wore when he broke down the cardboard boxes. They usually hung on the nail against the wall above the floor freezer, but this morning they were gone. George sat at his desk on the landing, his face buried in a newspaper.

"Where's the gloves?"

"What do you need 'em for?"

"The ice. Doc says I gotta wear 'em."

"Don't got 'em no more."

Webb walked back into the store and stared at the ice. He could see the outline of George's head in the dark window.

He went to the front door and walked outside. It was raining lightly as he climbed the hill to his apartment.

He went inside and found a pair of wool mitts in a drawer. He pulled them on. He walked back to the store where George stood waiting for him. He reached into the display case and began breaking the ice.

"What do you think you're doing?"

Webb kept his eyes fixed on the task.

"Take those goddamn things off."

Webb continued working.

George raised his cane and poked Webb in his side, jabbing his ribs. A sharp pain went to his brain and Webb's hand shot out, grabbing the tip of the cane and twisting it until the stick fell from his boss's hand. George stepped forward with his arm out, but Webb raised the cane over his head and the old man ducked, cowering. He saw the look in Webb's eyes and cried out before losing his balance and falling to the floor. Webb let the cane drop to his side.

"Give me my stick." The old man tried to stand, but slipped and fell back down. He stuck out his hand. Webb put out his gloved hand and lifted the old man to his feet. He handed George his cane.

"You're going back to prison," said George. Webb loosened his grip, and George yanked himself away. "Now hand me those gloves." Webb slid the gloves from his hands. "Get back to work." George stuffed the gloves into his hip pocket and hobbled back to the stock room.

Webb stared at the ice. He reached in, grabbed a large frozen hunk and snapped it in two.

50

Alice woke up next to him.

It was Sunday morning. The sun shone through the window. They sat across from each other eating banana pancakes.

After breakfast they walked down the hill. A Halloween display of cornhusks and jack-o-lanterns decorated the window of the bank. They planned to go to a matinee but when they stepped into the sun she suggested they go for a walk. A path of wood shavings followed next to the river into the forest. Frogs croaked in the bulrushes and crickets made rhythmic, high-pitched squeaks. Webb pointed to a clearing framed by a line of silver birches shimmering in the sunlight. "I used to catch salmon here. We'd cook 'em over a fire. The old mills up river dumped their waste. Can't eat 'em anymore."

When Alice thought of their fight earlier in the week, it seemed settled, and when he stopped to tie his shoelace, she placed a hand on his shoulder. Ducks dunked their heads, preening and honking. A young couple walked past. The woman smiled at Alice. Alice smiled back. As she continued walking she didn't turn to see if the couple was watching them.

"What did you do in prison?"

"I worked in the kitchen for an Italian man, Giuseppe. He snuck in crabmeat and grilled it with mushrooms for the men. He used to say a good meal was the last democratic opportunity left in this country. One morning they caught him sneaking in Parmesan cheese and fired him."

"Did you ever see him again?"

"Once. He brought me a bar of Swiss chocolate. I made it last a week."

"Giuseppe cared about you," she said.

Webb looked at her. Her face was pale, the blood drained from her cheeks.

"You okay?"

"I feel dizzy." She looked for a place to sit. Everything was damp. She pressed her face into his shoulder.

A couple approached from behind. Alice waited until they were out of earshot, and then sighed. "Sorry about that." She wiped her eyes with her sleeve. "What was your wife's name?"

"Karen."

"Was she pretty?"

"She was. And she had a real mouth on her." He smiled.

"What happened?"

He looked at her. "I don't know what happened. I really don't. We were so young."

"Did you love her?"

He nodded. "I still do."

A clapboard cottage with a narrow wraparound deck sat on the water's edge. A white sign with gold letters read: Whitehorse Restaurant. Webb stood with his hands in his pockets, studying the menu in the window. "It's been here since I was a kid."

"Have you eaten here?"

He shook his head.

She held his arm. "Maybe we should come here sometime."

A hawk flew lazy circles in the distance. A light rain began to fall.

"We should turn back," he said.

The rain fell harder, but they continued slowly.

They emerged from the woods, and crossed the street holding hands, and when they reached the hotel, she felt disoriented, as if what she had been doing was no longer possible. She stood before him outside the hotel and they held each other.

"I have to go upstairs," she said.

51

She climbed into bed wearing a sweater and jeans. She listened to the steady rattle of rainwater on the tin gutters outside her window. When she awoke it was dark. She went into the hallway and knocked on Ruth's door but there was no answer. She looked at the unfinished hollow wooden door and shook her head at the notion that it provided security.

"Ruth?"

A moment later Ruth opened the door and pulled her inside.

"There is something really wrong with me," said Alice. "It's so deep I don't know what it is, but it wants to bring me down."

"I'm listening, honey," said Ruth, pressing her lips together and applying lipstick in the mirror. "I just have to get ready for work."

Alice sat on the bed and fell backwards. "A year ago at a dinner party he told everyone about his vasectomy. It shouldn't have mattered. We agreed, no kids. When I asked why he hadn't mentioned it to me before, he dodged it. Said he got it done on the road so we wouldn't have to wait to screw. He wanted to know why it mattered. I'm his wife."

A car honked outside. Ruth went to the window. "I'm comin', Ricky."

"Webb was in prison," said Alice. "Did you know that?"

"Yeah, I heard something about that."

"Do you know what he did?"

Ruth looked at her. "Why don't you ask him?"

"I'm afraid he might have killed somebody."

Ricky blared his horn again. "Sweetheart, I gotta go." She grabbed Alice by the shoulders. "You're gonna be fine. Just stop being crazy and go talk to him."

*   *   *

For a moment, before Webb's door opened, Alice thought she could run. Get as far away as possible. But her feet didn't move. She would talk to him. She would ask him. But when the door opened she fell into him.

*   *   *

She sat naked on the bed with a pad of paper from his desk drawer propped on her lap. She sketched him as he appeared at the bathroom door with a towel around his waist and steam rising off his skin. "Don't move," she said. He was about to speak, but when he met her eyes, he stopped. The heater sputtered. She studied him closely, the thickness of his neck, the stiffness in his shoulders and the hardness of his stomach. She shaded in the glass-like wound on his forearm. The thunder cracked. The rain pounded against the window.

"I could have showered outside," he said.

"You're beautiful," she whispered.

He let the towel fall away as she continued to draw him, his scrotum relaxed, his penis soft and thick. The thunder rattled the room. The rain came in waves, battering the window and then retreating. She studied him carefully, the heft of his thighs, the tapering of his arms to his strong, square hands. He opened a drawer and began to get dressed. "Did you kill someone?" she asked. "Is that what you did?"

He sat at his desk and stared at the floor.

He didn't lift his eyes. He squeezed them shut and nodded. "Yeah."

When he looked up, she was looking at him. Her eyes were clear. "But you're not that person anymore."

He shook his head slowly.

She stared at her sketch for a long time. And then she began to fill him in with her pencil.

52

It was dark outside. Webb listened to the solitary plop of water landing in the metal bucket from the leaky roof. He sat behind the register, staring at the darkness. The floor lay unswept. There was produce to clean and dry goods to stock, but Webb sat behind the register staring at the street, watching the morning lighten by degrees.

George's truck rumbled down the alley. His brakes squealed and Webb was jolted from his reverie. He walked back to the stockroom and pushed on the side door. He waited at the back of the truck. George climbed out of the truck followed by a burly black dog that landed hard on the pavement. It walked in a tight circle before seeing Webb and lunging with a snarl.

"Pearl!" George slapped his hands, and the dog huffed back to her owner.

Webb reached in and pulled out the day's catch.

"Got some sea bass today," said George. "They wanted to give it to the rigs, but I brought Pearl, made 'em do the right thing."

He followed Webb inside and climbed the steps to the landing.

Webb brought in the rest of the fish before returning to the stock room and filling the case with ice. After his third trip to the stock room he heard George behind him, slowly descending the steps. The old man made his way up the aisle, holding Pearl tight on a leash. He stopped on the other side of the display case. "Goddamn roof. What's that gonna cost me?" he said. "Get goin' with that ice."

"Doc says I got arthritis."

"That's from jacking off thirty years. Crippled your hands."

Webb glanced at the dog, straining against the leash. He shook his head. "I can't do it anymore."

"Do your goddamn job."

"No."

George blinked. "Go stock the shelves." He threw Webb a set of keys. Webb tried to catch them, but he couldn't close his hands fast enough. He picked them off the floor and walked back to the stock room and into the alley where the rain fell hard. He opened the iron-barred door and walked down the concrete steps into the cellar. He heard splashing. When he turned on the light, he saw water shooting through a crack in the wall and saw the glow from the bare light bulb reflected in the black water splashing on the floor. He dipped his hand into the cold water and felt a tingle through his fingers to his elbow.

53

George stood halfway up the stairs of the cellar watching Hank McLean inspect his pump. "It's an old one," said Hank. "It's seen better days." Hank was a serious man with a thick head of reddish-brown hair who ran McLean Plumbing and Heating out of a cinderblock building on the edge of town. He placed the tote tray on his lap and removed a flat-blade screwdriver and wire brush. "They don't last forever." He scraped out the crack where the water was coming in and started cleaning it with a rag.

George folded his arms across his chest while Webb waded into the water, grabbing at stray cans floating on the surface. He placed them on the upper level. Cardboard boxes filled with canned goods lay at the bottom of the flood.

Hank mixed marine apoxy between his thumb and forefinger, twisting the separate black and white clays until they were a soft gray ball in his hands.

"It's a good pump," said George.

"George, this is not something I can fix. It's been in the

mud too long. The armature's shot, the impeller's rusted shut." He pressed the ball into the crack and began sealing it with a one-inch putty knife.

"It just needs a new armature."

Hank wiped the rag over the metal tag. "See this? It's a Bell and Gosset. They stopped making them years ago. I'd have to order parts from San Francisco, and you're not going to want to pay for 'em." He held up the pipe. "The whole thing is rusted through."

Webb's legs grew numb as he waded in the water up to his waist. His thoughts kept returning to his date that night with Alice. He called the Whitehorse the night before and made reservations. "For two," he said, and then said his name. There was a silence, and then the woman said, "We'll see you at seven-thirty."

"You can snake the pipe," said George.

"I can't. It's got holes. It discharges and just leaks right back in. If you want me to do it, we're doing it right. We need to move the discharge drain out toward the alley, and then we need to cement it right up to the exterior wall. You've got no rain gutter. This water just keeps going back in. That's why you have this problem in the first place."

"How much is a pump?"

"George, you're not hearing me. We're not talking about a pump here."

"I am hearing you!"

Hank sighed. "Lookit, I told you, the pump is one-fifty, but then we gotta . . ."

"Pump the water out and let me think about . . ."

"All my rental pumps are out. The whole town is having this problem." Hank was looking in the fuse box with his flashlight. "There's a flood at the bowling alley. The Pastime's got one. I got four basements I'm taking care of, that's why I'm saying, let me give you a fresh pump, right out of the box, and then at least you'll be in the dry."

George stared at the rusted old pump.

"How many appliances do you have?" asked Hank.

"Fridge, cooler, and freezer."

"You don't even have circuit breakers in here." He pulled out a fuse that had been wrapped in tinfoil. "What's this?"

George turned away guiltily.

"You wrapped 'em in tinfoil and screwed 'em back in? Cripes, I guess you don't blow too many fuses now, huh George?"

"Just give me the pump."

Hank walked along the edge of the cellar and climbed into the crawlspace, shining his flashlight at the porcelain spools nailed to the framing, connecting the copper wires. "You know you got bell and tooth wiring?"

"I don't know," said George.

"They're insulated with cloth." Hank crawled back out. "Those are live wires, George. Do you know how hot they get? This is a code violation. If the inspector sees this...heck, I can't install a pump in here even if I want to. Not 'til you update this wiring. I'll lose my license. There's no ground on this receptacle. Webb coulda been electrocuted."

"Just put the pump in."

Hank closed his tote tray and began walking up the stairs. "You haven't heard a word I said, George."

"Where you going?" asked George.

"Every time you call, I tell you what you need and you send me away. This building is a firetrap. This whole block could go up from this. Damn it, George, you're the richest man in town and you'll have a blue dwarf before you pay anyone what they're worth. When you're ready to do the job right, give me a call." He walked up the steps and out into the rain.

Webb stood in the water, staring up at his boss.

"We're going to have to bail it," said George to Webb. "There's some buckets in the stock room." George clapped his hands together. "Let's go."

"I have to stop at six."

"Why? What do you have to do?"

"I gotta be somewhere."

"You got a date."

Webb said nothing.

George smiled. "You'll work till it's done."

54

Alice waited for Webb in the lobby. She wore a periwinkle dress underneath her raincoat. She glanced at her watch and after twenty minutes went to the front door and looked up the street to see if he was on his way. A couple of men stood outside the Pastime smoking cigarettes. She popped open her umbrella and, resisting the urge to run, crossed the street slowly as the rain fell around her.

The Pastime was choked with patrons, mostly men in flannel shirts and plastic coats. A couple of waitresses in tight jeans and T-shirts served them drinks. Behind the bar a flat-screen TV played a hockey game, and at the back of the room a moose head was nailed to a wall. A mirror ball hung from the peak of an A-frame over what presumably was a dance floor.

Near the back of the room, Lester sat with a group of men. She ordered a drink at the bar and listened to him talk about how the framers of the amendment used the indefinite article "a" not "the" referring not to a specific *well-regulated militia* but to the idea that militias comprised of citizens bearing arms are necessary to secure a free state. She glanced at the worn wooden surface of the bar. A brass plate screwed into the wood read:

Bud's spot 1922-2004
He went too soon.

A moment later Lester sat next to her. "Mind if I join you?"

"Not at all," she said. "Just don't tell me you're in the NRA."

"Uh-uh," he said. "Town's too small. Can't afford to isolate my allegiance. Though I am a member of the LSAS."

"What's that?"

"Lawyer's Second Amendment Society. We support the individual's right to bear arms."

"What's the difference?"

"We *support* it," he said, sitting on a stool and signaling the bartender.

"Ah, clever."

"Half these guys believe the Constitution is a hoax. Welcome to Waiden, home of the moderate extremists, conspiracy theorists and big-hearted bigots. Tell you one thing though, they're not dumb. See that guy in the brown jacket? That's Winston. He prints his own driver's license and believes he's exempt from state law. I asked him once if he paid taxes. He looked at me, straight-faced: 'To who?'" Lester laughed. "These are my clients."

The bartender poured him another beer. Lester raised his glass. "To the prettiest girl in the room." She took a sip. "So, what's up? No date tonight?" She stopped smiling.

"Don't do that."

He glanced around the room, as if he was looking for reinforcement. Her hand shook as she reached for her beer.

"So, why did you leave your husband?"

"I'm not sure I have a good answer for that."

"Really? Usually people are dying to tell you what a loser their ex is."

"He's definitely not a loser. Not by most definitions."

"No," he laughed. "I gathered that."

"What does that mean?"

"Well . . ." He studied her, then pursed his lips. "I mean, you are missus Chick Wolfson. Right?"

She blinked. "How did you know that?"

"I'm sorry. Were you enjoying your anonymity?"

"Kind of. Yeah."

"We're in the Internet age. There's not much left, I'm afraid. I hope you're not upset."

She shrugged. "It's not a big deal."

"You were married for . . . ?"

"Thirteen years."

"Stubborn."

"Yup." She sipped her beer.

Lester squinted. "So we're not going to trash our exes?"

"I made a mistake. A very long mistake."

"That's awfully mature. I want to hear what you have to say about him after you've had a beer."

"I actually have to go," she said.

"Wait." He looked at her, about to speak.

She knew where it was going and she didn't want to hear it. She slid off her stool. "I gotta go." He reached for her but she pulled away.

She ran back across the street to the hotel. The lobby was empty. A light flickered under Milo's office door. A sitcom played on the television. Alice listened to the rise and fall of the canned laughter. There was something hypnotic about the laugh track, its rhythmic predictability, as if the rest of the world was in on some private joke. She didn't want to go to her room. She went back out into the rain. Water ran down the sidewalk, soaking through her shoes. She climbed the hill to Webb's building and went inside. She knocked on his door. Across the hall, a man peeked out. She gave him a look and he closed his door. She was about to knock again, but changed her mind and walked back outside. As she strode past the general store she heard the splash of water hitting pavement in the alley. She glanced back in time to see a second geyser fly out from the alcove onto the pavement.

She crept into the alley. As she approached the alcove she saw a figure, naked to the waist, standing in the doorway behind the iron-gate, his body streaked with mud and sweat. He held a five-gallon bucket in each hand. He looked at her, eyes haunted, and reached into his pocket, handing her a key. "There's a key in his desk drawer. It's brass. It'll open this."

She opened the door to the stock room. It was impeccably ordered and smelled of freshly cut wood. She dropped her umbrella at the door and climbed the six steps up George's landing to his desk. She pulled open the middle drawer. Moving away some loose papers she saw a set of keys, snatched them and went back outside. She didn't bother opening her umbrella as she ducked into the alley. She pushed a key into the slot and opened the gate.

"There was a flood," he said.

"Did you get locked in?"

He looked at her strangely. His face screwed up as she reached for him. The bucket fell from his bloody hand and bounced back down the steps into the cellar.

*　*　*

Alice sat on the edge of Webb's bed in her coat. He emerged

from the bathroom, a towel around his waist.

"I want to kill him," she said.

He sat next to her and took her hand but there was a distance between them.

*   *   *

She couldn't feel him as they lay together. "Please. You at least need to go to your parole officer," she said.

"All I think about lately is how you're gonna leave," he said. "I wonder if you're gonna tell me, or if I'm just gonna wake up and you'll be gone."

"I'm not going to leave," she said.

55

George was at the counter waiting on a customer when Webb pushed open the door. The display case was stocked with fish, a thick layer of ice beneath it. Webb walked past George to the stock room where he noticed the gloves hanging from the nail. He touched them. They were still wet.

At five o'clock, Alice entered the general store in her uniform. George watched her from the open door of the stock room and he called to Webb. "Cooley, you were gonna bring that rice up an hour ago."

Alice glared at George. Webb looked at her, and then at his boss. George began walking up the aisle, his face rigid. "That means now, Cooley." Webb excused himself. George stood halfway between the back door and Alice, his body tilted forward on his cane.

"Why do you talk to him like that?"

A thin smile flickered on George's face.

"He's a human being," she said.

"Human being," said the old man. He smiled. Alice could

see the flicker of malice underneath the worn skin. He moved toward her, like he was smelling her. "Webb Cooley went to prison," he said. She wanted to run. "Did he tell you what he did?"

Alice stood transfixed. She shook her head.

"He killed his wife."

Bile pushed at the back of her throat. The old man stepped closer, the rasp in his voice gone, replaced by a sweet smoothness. "He didn't tell you about the iron, did he? How he smashed her head in, out there in his trailer with all them other trash. Bashed in her skull, brains spilling out of her head." The old man grunted a laugh. "How can I speak to him like that? Cops out there every night. Reading about 'em in the paper every Monday morning." He inched toward her, but she could no longer distinguish the distance. "Cops found him three days later, lying on his couch, watching TV." The old man was standing in front of her now. "He's a reptile."

Webb appeared from the stock room, carrying a box filled with bags of rice. He met her glance from over George's shoulder. Her eyes were blank.

She heard herself ask him if it was true. Webb looked at George, and so did Alice, expecting the old man to laugh cruelly, to say it was all a joke. But he said nothing.

"Webb?" she asked. "Is it true?"

He nodded his head. He saw it in her eyes, a click. He watched himself get canceled.

"You killed your wife?" She said it out loud to hear how it sounded.

"Alice," he said.

But her eyes were haunted, poisoned by George's words. George pivoted on his cane and looked at Webb.

Webb wanted to scream, to pull her back to him, but he

couldn't move. The box slipped from his hands. Rice sprayed across the floor. She backed away, half-turned, and kept moving toward the door. She heard her name, and she moved faster.

"Goddamn it," shouted George. "Clean that shit up."

"I want to talk to you," said Webb.

"No." She shook her head. "I can't," she said. "Alice."

She ran out of the store into the rain.

"Clean up that rice," said George, but Webb was already moving out the door after her.

The rain fell heavily, the cold cutting through her uniform. She couldn't feel it. He chased after her. He grabbed her arm. She screamed at him. "Don't touch me."

Heads turned. Faces watched from behind windows across the street. "I want to talk to you."

"Take your hands off me."

He stood in front of her, but she couldn't see him anymore. "Please. Alice."

She walked into the hotel.

Across the street, diners watched as he walked back up the hill.

He entered the store. He walked past George, back to the stock room. A knife sat atop the butcher block. He grabbed it, blood rushing through his brain. He pushed the flimsy metal door. It made a loud whack as it smashed into the back wall.

The man examining apples in the corner dropped his basket, grabbed his wife's hand and pulled her toward the door.

George stood at the register. Webb walked slowly up the aisle, gripping the knife. He stood opposite George, the counter between them. George had a look in his eye, like he was pleased. "You're nothing," he said. "A reptile."

Webb stared into George's eyes. And then he blinked. The old man wanted him to do it.

A fly buzzed between them. Webb's breath slowed. He placed the knife on the counter and walked out into the street.

56

"Collect call," Alice whispered to the operator. She shivered against the hotel lobby's heater. Cliff's uniform was starting to itch, and the fetid smell of wet Polyester made her stomach weak. Out the window she watched a group of teenagers standing in a loose circle across the street. Two of the boys wore T-shirts, oblivious to the cold. One of them lit a cigarette. Facing away from Alice, slightly apart from the others stood a young girl in a long green coat. She was small. With her hood up and hands stuffed deeply into her pockets, she looked like a little boy.

The phone rang twice before her mother answered.

"Oh God. We've been terrified." She called to her husband. "Joe, it's Alice."

"Mom, I told you I was okay."

"I've called you a hundred times."

"I broke my cell phone."

"Who does something like this? What is the matter with you?"

"I'm sorry."

"We thought you were dead or in a cult or something."

"I'm okay," said Alice.

"Oh, praise God."

She heard her father in the background demanding the phone.

"Why didn't you call me? I'm your mother," she said. "Joe, let me talk to her."

Alice watched one of the boys pass the cigarette to the girl next to him, a tomboy with short hair and the cuffs of her jeans stuffed into the top of her boots.

"I think there's something wrong with me."

"There's nothing wrong with you, honey. You're just going through something. You're going to come home and we're going to straighten this out."

"Straighten what out?"

She heard her father in the background demanding the phone.

"Joe, just give me a second. Everything, sweetheart."

"Mom, I don't know what I'm doing."

"We've talked to Chick. He wants you to come home."

"That's not what I mean. I don't want to go back to him. I don't love him. I never did. It was a stupid marriage. It was a stupid, childish mistake."

"But he's your hubby."

"No. He's not my hubby. I'm not going back to him."

"We'll talk about it when you come home. Now just tell me what happened."

She watched the girl in the green coat, her ankle twisted anxiously as the boy next to her offered her the cigarette. Alice held her breath. The hood of the girl's coat shook slightly. She waved the cigarette away. Across the lobby, a couple of mill workers stood at the bottom of the stairs talking loudly. "I met someone," she said. "He just got out of prison."

"Oh, Alice. Oh, God," she said. "What was he in prison for?"

One of the boys flicked the cigarette into the street and Alice watched the ember die in the gutter. They walked down the hill past the bank, the girl in the coat trailing as they disappeared around the corner. Alice wanted to follow them, warn them of something, but she didn't know what.

"You won't understand."

"Sweetheart, I'll understand."

"He killed his wife," she whispered.

Trish screamed.

"Alice, you have to get out of there," said her father. "I'm coming to get you. Where are you?"

"Alice, you have to come home."

"Trish, get off the line," said Joe. "Now Alice, you either need to come up here, or I'm coming down to get you. Okay?"

"Okay."

"Which?"

"I'll come up."

She had never heard fear in her father's voice before. "Alice, we want you to come up right now. Get in the car and we'll stay on the phone."

"Dad, I'm not going back to Chick."

"That's fine. I understand. Whatever you want. We just want you out of there. We want you safe."

"I am safe. That's not the problem."

"What is the problem?"

"The problem is that I can't count on myself."

Her father sighed. "I understand."

"Do you? Do you really?"

"Of course he does," said Trish.

"Trish," said Joe. "Get off the line."

"Tell her you understand, Joe. For God's sakes, just tell her."

"If you give me a goddamn second."

"I can talk to my daughter too if I want. She's my daughter too, Joe."

"Trish, for Christ sakes . . ."

"And don't tell me what to do! I'll goddamn talk to her if I goddamn want!"

Her father was breathing heavily. "One second, Alice," he said. She heard them in the background. "You're not sticking to the plan. We just want to get her up here. The therapist said . . ."

"I don't care what she said," said Trish. "It's a stupid plan."

"She's lost her fucking mind."

"Dad?"

"What?"

"I haven't lost my mind."

"I know that. Of course not. That's not what I meant."

"Did you talk to a therapist about me?"

"We were concerned."

"I'm going to be okay, Dad. I know this is hard for you guys, but I'll call you soon."

"Wait. Alice."

"I love you. I'll call you soon."

The street was empty. It was dark outside. She stared at the receiver, with its nicks and claw marks. She climbed the stairs to her room.

57

Webb walked through the cemetery until he reached a small headstone with the inscription:

Karen Parks

1974 - 1993

In Loving Memory

Parks was her maiden name and her family made sure she rested with it. Webb told the judge he didn't remember what he did. His lawyer explained to the jury that it was a crime of passion, committed in the throes of an alcoholic blackout, but the truth was he did remember.

His father called that morning, before Webb went to work at the mill, asked for thirty dollars to buy a tire for his truck. Karen overheard the call. "You hate the prick, but you're going to give him more money?"

"I don't want to hear it." He pulled his overalls over a thermal shirt.

"How are we going to cover March?"

"I'll take care of it."

"Shhh. Earl's still sleeping," she said. She followed him into the living room where her fifteen-year-old brother lay on the couch, wiping sleep from his eyes. "Webb, I swear, you give him any more of our money, I'll kill you."

"Then do it," he said. "Earl, you want some breakfast?"

"Coffee," said Earl, running a hand through his hair.

Webb drove Earl home in his Cutlass. He cracked open a pack of smokes and knocked one out before handing the pack to Earl. They smoked in silence as Webb pulled up to the curb. Earl's mother held back the curtains, watched them from the front room.

"Going to school today?" asked Webb, blowing a stream of smoke out the window.

Earl glanced at his mother. "Guess so," he said, taking another drag. He watched her close the curtains.

"She hates me," said Webb.

"Don't like me neither."

Earl stabbed out his cigarette in the ashtray and climbed out of the car.

Webb didn't know why he drove to his father's house. They were two months behind on rent, and with groceries, cigarettes, beer, gas for two cars, they were in trouble. Karen worked part-time as a cashier in Indiola at an adult bookstore called ADULT BOOKS.

He remembered when things weren't like this, remembered the wedding in the trailer park community room, remembered looking into the eyes of his bride and knowing it was right. He remembered crying when he made his speech, sorry his mother wasn't alive to be there. Percy was his best man, proud and solemn. He remembered the honeymoon at the motel on Gold Beach in the room overlooking the ocean, and falling asleep with the balcony door open so they could hear the surf.

It was his nineteenth summer, the summer he and Karen picked up Shelly on weekends and drove to the beach. He saw that Shelly had a secret; there was a moment of hesitation, like she was searching for signs of what it looked like to still be innocent. It was the summer he and Karen were blind for each other, before their limitations roared from nowhere to ambush them.

Webb pulled into his father's driveway, a single lane of dirt covered by a couple wheelbarrow loads of gravel. His father stood on the porch in yellow boxers, barrel-bellied, hulking shoulders, cigarette dangled from his lips. "Did you bring it?"

"Where's Shelly?"

"Sleepin'."

"I wanna see her."

"Said she's sleepin'."

Gus Cooley stepped in front of Webb, blocking the door. Webb was young and confused. His suspicion embarrassed him. Gus shoved his palm in Webb's face. Webb reached into his back pocket, and then hesitated. "You gonna drive her to school?"

"Sure." Gus smirked. "Where is it?"

"I didn't bring it."

Gus' truck listed on its front flat tire. He winced. "What have you got?"

"Nothing."

He grabbed Webb, shoved his hand into his son's pocket and pulled out his wallet. He snatched the cash, all of it.

"You said thirty bucks."

"I'm keepin' it, you lying sack of shit." He shoved Webb in the chest. Webb tripped backwards and fell off the porch. When he stood up, his father was back in the house.

"Open the door." He screamed. He banged on the window. And then he stopped. Just stopped. He couldn't do it.

It was too painful to name what he believed was happening. It would make it real. As long as he didn't know what it was, there was hope. He could live in that place where nothing was happening.

He pulled out of the driveway. Instead of turning right toward the mill, he drove to the liquor store and put a bottle on his card. He sat in his car and drank until the Pastime opened. He thought about his sister. When he took her to the ocean, she was different. He remembered her squeal as she ran to the water, and how it stopped short, as if she'd lost permission. He remembered dropping her off and how she hugged Karen, clung to her before she walked carefully toward the house.

It was early and Webb was the only patron. He sat across from Manny, a leather-face Irishman who stood reading *The Oregonian*. Webb came in regularly for the past couple years. Sometimes he came alone, and sometimes with Percy, the two sat at the bar making cheap bets over car specs and then finding their answers in a drag-racing magazine. Webb tapped the bar with his shot glass and Manny poured him another. He drank until he no longer saw his father walking back into the house and shutting the door, until he didn't have to think about his sister and what he felt helpless to prevent.

"Looks like you've seen better days," said Manny.

"My old man's sick," said Webb.

"It's when we lose our fathers we become men."

Webb nodded. He didn't explain that his father wasn't sick like that. "What happens when we lose our mothers?"

Manny poured another shot. "We become orphans."

Webb pulled up to the trailer and saw Karen's Ford parked out front. He sat in the car and took a breath. He needed to cool down. She shoved herself out the front door and charged at his car. Rapped on his window. "Get out, you sorry piece of shit."

He stared at her through the glass. Her eyes were wild. "Go back in the house," he said.

"Get outta the car or I'll smash the window."

His eyes fell to the iron in her hand. The air was cool and steam rose from the metal. She raised the iron, about to strike. He opened the door and climbed out. "Don't do that."

She saw the paper bag in his hand. "You been drinking?"

"Outta my way." He pushed past her.

"Where's our check? Hey! I'm talking to you." She grabbed his shirt from the back and it came off in her hands.

He walked into the house and down the hall. He shut the bedroom door, locked it. He sat on the bed and drank from the bottle. She kicked open the door.

"I said, where's the money? Answer me."

He took a swig.

"Did you give it to him?"

"Go away. You don't understand." He screamed. He didn't see her as she propelled herself across the room. She pummeled him. He made a fist and threw it against her cheek. She fell to the floor, stunned, then jumped to her feet and ran out of the room. Burying his face in his hands, he felt adrenalin pound through him. He heard the footsteps and looked up in time to turn his body and avoid the sharp end of the iron as it flew at his chest. He raised his forearm and caught the force of the metal. It seared his skin. He roared. She ran at him again, dove onto him, pounded him with her fists. He grabbed her wrists but she opened her mouth and clamped down on his cheek. Warm blood trickled into his mouth. He reached back and his fingers slipped neatly through the handle of the iron.

His brain did funny things with what happened next. For years he told himself he didn't remember. But that wasn't true. He did. Part of him played it over in his head while another part told him it was a dream. He raised his hand and brought it down, slammed the iron into her temple. It happened fast. There was barely time to make a decision. Barely. A part of him tried to convince another part there was no time to think. Crime of passion, said his lawyer.

But another part was aware of the moment, that fraction of a second when a decision was made. Even with all the alcohol, the fire in his eyes, he knew what he was doing, and for a fraction of a second he didn't care. He couldn't be sure, but he believed the reason he brought his hand down had nothing to do with her. The iron he slammed into her temple wasn't meant for her. It was meant simply to end this *thing,* whatever it was, this *thing* they had, that all of them had, or that had them, this *thing* that wasn't going away, that was infecting everything.

He lay still, his wife limp on top of him, her blood dripping onto his face, mingling with his own. The iron slipped from his fingers and he slid out from under her. He gazed at her balanced precariously on the edge of the mattress and slid his arms through hers, moving her gently to the middle of the bed. He used to fear her scrutiny, afraid that she might discover everything he was trying to hide from her, that he was worthless and inept. Now he let his eyes linger on hers. The left side of her head was caved-in, her hair matted, wet and glistening. A fine scarlet mist sprayed across the sheets of their unmade bed. A shallow pool of blood collected in a fold, and when he shifted his position, it leaked to the edge, dripping onto the scuffed linoleum encircling his bottle. He picked the bottle up, and as he sipped, he watched the circle slowly fill with blood.

He checked for a pulse, but there was none. There was no need to call the authorities, he reasoned, and so he went to the living room and continued to drink.

The next day, Percy came over and they sat in his car and smoked and talked about cars. When Karen failed to appear at work on Monday, her boss called the police.

"She's in the bedroom," Webb told the officers who knocked on his door. They found her lying on her back on the bed, arms at her sides, her head resting on the pillow.

He didn't resist when they arrested him. He surrendered gratefully, relieved he would no longer be a danger to others.

Percy became a witness for the prosecution, telling the court how they sat in his car for hours, *shootin' the breeze* and smoking weed. He told the court how Webb explained to him that they couldn't go inside because Karen was in a foul mood. The prosecutor called Webb deranged, ruthless, unimaginably cold-blooded. It was Percy's testimony that horrified the jury and put Webb away for twenty years.

*　*　*

He stared at his late wife's grave. He wanted to speak to her, tell her it scared him how easily it all happened, that he feared this blind spot, that perhaps Lester was right, that twenty years was not enough.

The parole board had asked him if he was ready to return to civilization. He had lied. He had told them he was a new man. But he wasn't. He was exactly the same. They had called him a model prisoner but that was because when he was inside there was no one to love. The rage had returned when he met this woman, and only now was he aware of his grotesque secret: he was incapable of love. He used to see it in the other men, the haunted madness in their eyes, men so hungry for love that they tore people apart in search of it.

He didn't want to belong to these men. He wanted to be ordinary, even though he knew it was too late for that.

58

"What did you think he was in for, selling spliffs?" Ruth sat across from Alice in their back booth at Corky's.

"You're not shocked by this?"

"Course I'm shocked. Course I am. It's shocking." She spooned a large scoop of ice cream into her mouth. "I just sort of figured it was something. I remember I dated this one guy, he never murdered his wife, but I'm pretty sure he killed somebody." She gazed at the plywood ceiling. "What the hell was his name? Barry, I think. But I had to call him Dan."

"You think I'm crazy to be upset by this?"

"Heck, I don't know. Maybe I just seen a little more of the world than you, but I do think you're wrapped a little tight sittin' there like he's gonna sneak up on you with an ice pick or somethin.'"

Alice took a sip of tea and shook her head. "I don't think you understand what I'm talking about."

Pie crust fell from Ruth's lip and disappeared somewhere into the folds of her sweat pants. "What are you afraid of?"

Alice leaned forward for emphasis. "He killed his wife."

Ruth's tongue reached for something along the upper ridge of her mouth. "I know. You said that."

Alice stared outside.

"Phyllis, how 'bout another?" said Ruth, holding up her plate.

"Apple?"

"Got any cobbler?"

"A la mode?"

"Why not?"

Ruth placed her fork on the plate. "I never heard you say nuthin' bad about him. He don't hit you. He don't drink. He got a job. You got the holy trinity right there."

They sat in silence watching the rain hit the glass.

Phyllis placed the cobbler in front of Ruth.

"Thanks, angel."

Alice watched a woman walking down the street holding the hand of her young son. The boy looked up at his mother, listening as she gestured with her hands, explaining something to him. A pickup truck pulled up to the Frontier Hotel. "Ah shit, there's Ricky," said Ruth. The horn blared. Ruth sniffed and wiped her nose.

"Tell him to go to hell," said Alice.

Ricky hopped out of his truck and stood under Ruth's window, shouting her name.

"He looks like a rat. Look at him. I wonder how long he'll stand there."

"Forever," said Ruth. "You gonna be okay?"

"No."

"You know, you coulda asked him, if it was so goddamn serious. You coulda asked him what he was in for."

Alice stared at Ruth. The table trembled, and she realized

Ruth was bouncing her foot on the metal base.

"What?" asked Ruth.

"Nothing."

"Don't say that. I'm not some imbecile who don't understand what you're talking about. What were you gonna say?"

"He killed his wife," said Alice, slowly. "Where I'm from that's *red flag*."

Ruth watched Ricky standing under the window shouting her name. "But that was twenty years ago," said Ruth.

The tea burned Alice's throat. "How did you know that?"

Ruth hesitated. "You told me," she lied.

"No," said Alice. "I sure did not."

Ruth watched Ricky Jewell reach through the window of his truck and press on the horn. "Everybody knows," said Ruth.

"You mean, how much time he served, or what he was in for?"

Ruth stared at her plate.

Alice's voice grew louder. "Why didn't you tell me?"

"You didn't ask."

"I did ask," said Alice. "Yes, I did."

Ruth's top lip was sweating. She sniffed. "Well then, what'd Webb say?"

"Nothing. He just said it was someone he knew."

"That's cause he was scared."

Alice glanced around the room. She recognized a woman sitting with her husband at the counter, a woman Alice had seen knitting in the circle at Joyce's. She suddenly felt embarrassed to be sitting with Ruth, and Ruth saw it too. Ruth wiped her fingers on the napkin and tore it apart. "I'm not a goddamn charity case," said Ruth, reaching into her purse. "I don't need this horseshit." She threw some bills onto the table. "You'll be lucky you ever find another friend like me." The couple watched Ruth hoist herself out of the booth. "I'm true blue. Right Phyllis?"

"Sure thing, Ruth."

Ruth barged out of the diner. She crossed the street, and Ricky turned to her. Alice watched something in Ruth withdraw as she motioned that she had to go upstairs to get her things. He shook his head and she climbed into the truck. Ricky looked at Alice through the window and she turned away. She stared around the restaurant. A song played quietly from the kitchen. It was "Alien Love." Chick was singing to her. She listened to his voice like she was searching for clues. She looked at her car parked across the street. He was eight hours away. All she had to do was climb in and she could be back with him.

She paid her bill and went out the door avoiding the woman's gaze at the counter. She didn't want to go back to her room, so she walked into the Pastime Tavern.

59

Alice strode past a hive of noisy drunken patrons to the bar. Lester sat next to an old man in a buckskin jacket. She tapped him on the shoulder. He turned casually and smiled. "What are you drinking?"

"Same as last time."

Lester ordered a beer and gestured to the man. "This is Plato, our mayor. Plato, this is Alice."

The old man had hawkish eyes and silver hair. "What's a fine looking woman like you talking to this deadbeat for?"

She tried to smile. Lester held her shoulder. "What's up?"

She took a deep breath. "He killed his wife."

Lester closed his eyes. "Jesus Christ." He watched a kid make a shot at the pool table. He let out a low whistle. "So, now you know."

She gazed around the room. Men and women tilted toward each other, yelling into each other's faces while Hank Williams played on the jukebox. A couple do-si-do'd in the corner. "Now I know."

Plato slid off his stool and disappeared into the crowd. A man patted Lester on the back and continued unsteadily on his feet. "Full house tonight."

"How's the case?"

"It's over. We won."

Alice raised her glass. "Congratulations."

"Ned's on probation for a year. He's gonna take some anger management classes. Between me and you, he shoulda gone to jail."

"How did you manage that?"

"The Mexican's lawyer was an imbecile."

There was a sudden movement, a shift in the feel of the room. Alice glanced at the front door. Heads turned to watch Webb enter, eyes down, and take a seat at the bar.

"I'm gonna go," she said to Lester.

"Stay and finish your drink."

"I can't." She slid off her stool.

"Tomorrow night, why don't you come over to my place? We'll have a little barbecue."

"I'm not up for that."

"For a hamburger?"

"For a date."

"Who said a date? I don't want to date you. No, we're buddies. Remember our deal? You're going to come over, hang out, see the view from my deck."

Alice watched Webb. He looked in her direction and she turned away. Lester's face darkened. "Here comes trouble," he said. She turned to see Webb standing in front of her.

"I want to talk to you," he said.

Lester stood. "Better leave her alone."

Webb held her gaze. "Did I change that much since this morning?"

Lester stuck a hand out between them. "She doesn't want to talk to you."

"I'm going home," she said. She walked away.

Webb turned after her but Lester grabbed him. Webb spun and took a swing, catching Lester on the chin.

Lester's head snapped back and a couple of men grabbed Webb and threw him against the bar. "Hey!"

Webb kicked and thrashed until half a dozen men had him boxed in, held him down. Webb sank to the floor. One of the men shouted not to move but he jerked and kicked.

They punched and kicked him.

"Leave him alone," said Lester. "That's enough." They stopped. They let him up and he sat down on a stool. His cheek was cut and he held his side.

"Give me a drink, Manny."

"I can't do that."

Lester sat next to him. "Let me buy you a soda."

Webb ignored him. "Give me a drink. I got as much right as anyone."

"Hell, give him a drink," said Lester. He placed five dollars on the bar.

"What'll you have?"

"Shot and a beer."

Manny poured a shot of Jack Daniels. Percy sat at the end of the bar, his eyes trained on the glass as Webb raised it to his lips. He watched Webb toss it back. Webb placed the glass on the bar and felt the warm burn in his gut. The tightness in his chest loosened. He exhaled before raising the pint and taking a long drink.

Lester put a hand on Webb's back and patted him. Webb could smell his cologne, woodsy and sweet. He wanted to slam Lester's round little face into the bar, but he did nothing.

He felt the alcohol seep into him, work its way into his veins, warming his body.

"There's more fish in the sea," said Lester.

Webb pretended to listen, pretended they were friends so he could keep drinking. He felt this thing getting activated, this urge for more. He stared at the liquor behind the bar and wished everyone was gone, that they were all dead and he could be alone in this room with all of this booze. He wanted to drink until he was numb, until his insides felt nothing.

"Gimme another, Manny."

"Pace yourself, brother. I'll give you another pint, but let's take our time, yeah?"

Webb nodded. Manny placed the drink on the bar. Webb stared at it. He inhaled. He tried counting to ten, but only made it to three before sucking half of it back.

"Hell yeah." Lester chuckled. "You are a thirsty son of gun."

A man stood behind Webb and poked his shoulder. "Remember me?" The last time he saw Karen's brother was at his sentencing. Earl was a kid then, a wiry teen with a lost look in his eyes. The man standing over him was a lumberjack, outweighing him by fifty pounds.

"Let's go outside," said Earl.

Men watched silently as Webb slid off the stool.

It was cold outside, but he felt hot, his T-shirt stuck to his skin. Earl directed Webb into the alley. An animal darted in front of them as they walked down the narrow passageway.

"That's far enough."

Earl grabbed Webb by the shoulders and pushed him against the wall. Some men watched from the corner of the building but disappeared when Earl removed the gun from inside his jacket and pressed the snout into Webb's forehead.

"You know how many times I've wanted to come into that

store and put this in your face?"

Webb gazed back at Earl, not breathing.

"I used to dream what it'd be like to see you dead. I had a guy who was gonna do it for me." Earl dropped the hammer. "I didn't care if I went to prison." He squinted at Webb from a broad, square face. Webb noticed he had his sister's eyes.

Webb's voice came out as a whisper. "Earl, put the gun down."

"Okay," he said. "But first I want something from you." he pushed the barrel hard into Webb's cheek. "I want you to bring my sister back." For a moment Webb saw a flash of hope in Earl's eyes, like when they were young and he believed Webb could do anything. He pressed harder. "You got ten seconds." He lifted a hand and smacked Webb across the face, opening a gash at the corner of his mouth. "Nine."

"I can't."

Earl pressed harder on the barrel. "Shut up."

Webb pursed his lips together. "Earl . . ."

Earl smacked him again. "I said, shut up."

Webb took a deep breath, inhaling the cold wet air. He remembered how the three of them drove to the ocean together when they needed to get away, smoked cigarettes and dug for clams. He remembered watching Earl during the sentencing, the confusion on his face that hardened into hatred. He squeezed his eyes shut. "Just do it." He felt the grit from the brick grind into the back of his head as Earl pushed hard with the gun.

"I'm gonna."

"I thought about you all the time."

"Shut up," said Earl.

"I wondered if you ever got that car, that black 'Cuda, remember?"

Webb's palms pressed hard against the wall.

Earl tightened on the trigger but something in his eyes remembered.

"I got married."

"You did?"

"We got a little girl. She's gonna be five."

"What's her name?"

"You're not my friend."

"I know," said Webb. "What's her name?"

Earl looked down the alley to the street. The neon sign glowed under the awning. Anger rose in him that his plan was failing. "Karen," he said. He fought something, like speaking her name brought her back and she was standing between them now, guiding her brother's gun down to his side. His brow furrowed and he stared at Webb, trying to speak, but all he could do was repeat his sister's name. Karen.

Webb reached out and put his arms around Earl. He held him and let the man cry. Earl's body shook.

"You're not my friend," said Earl.

"I'm sorry," said Webb, holding him tightly.

60

Webb stayed to the shoulder of the road, his face pressed into the wind, arms swinging hard at his sides. The cloud cover lifted and a new moon glistened off the pavement. He had cycled this road in his youth, but he'd never walked it at night. His senses remembered the landscape, how the fir trees gave way to brush and then, finally, just wild grass sprouting from the sand at the ocean. But he was still at the trees, striding hard through this dark corridor of freezing wind. He walked fast, trying to shake the voices pounding in his brain. *Worthless,* his father had said, and so he'd left the house and married the voice. *Give me the money, or I'll kill you.* He'd tried to silence it with force, but it only grew louder. *Back in your cages, men.* And after twenty years the voice employed him. *You're a worm, Cooley, barely human.* It lived inside him. He took long strides searching for an escape.

The headlights from the police car cast a pale glow off the mist. The car crawled next to him. John Smith leaned across the passenger seat and asked where he was going. "You got another nine miles to the coast, Webb. You're gonna freeze to death."

Webb ignored him and picked up his pace. John pulled ahead and parked on the shoulder. He opened his door as Webb walked past, breath shooting from his mouth in sharp puffs.

John jogged alongside him. "Hey, hold up a minute."

Webb stopped walking and John put his hands on his knees, breathing hard. "If I let you go, you know what they'll do to me?" he asked. "I gotta answer to Tripp."

Webb looked at the moon. "Don't put this on Tripp," he said, walking away.

"Hey." John chased after him. "I'm just doing my job. Tripp's gonna know by tomorrow, if somebody hasn't called her already."

"It's not Tripp," said Webb. "You're the law too." The trees loomed high on either side like advancing armies at a standstill.

"I know," said John. "You don't have to tell me that."

"Then stand up for yourself!" Webb's voice echoed.

John stepped back.

"What are you getting mad at me for? I'm trying to help you. If you keep going you're gonna give 'em a real good reason to put you back. Now c'mon. I got the heater on. Let me take you home."

John walked back to the car and climbed in. Webb stood on the road and watched him sit in the car, pretending to fiddle with the radio. Webb walked to the car. He opened the front passenger door but John asked him to ride in the back. Webb opened the back door and climbed in. "I don't know what happened to you tonight," said John. Webb stared at the mesh screen between them. The car smelled of French fries. "I know I'm the law," said John. "You don't have to tell me that." He punched the steering wheel. "Goddamn it." He did a U-turn, and then pulled over. "All right. Come on. Ride up front. I don't care about them."

Webb opened the door and got into the front seat.

"What'dya go into the Pastime for, anyway?" John asked, pulling onto the road.

Webb stared at the dashboard. "I don't know."

They drove in silence until John pulled up to the curb outside Webb's apartment.

John sighed. "I wish I knew what happened. All these years I still go over it in my head."

"You scared her," said Webb. He wanted to get out of the car.

"I never scared your sister," said John. "What did I do?"

Webb gazed up the hill into the darkness. When he listened to John talk about Shelly he hated himself for leaving her alone with their father. "You loved her," he said.

He saw John's face twitch, and then the reflection of water in his eye. He thought about Shelly living up the road, married to Harland, a man with his own ideas on marriage. "She's never coming back," said Webb. "Get that through your head."

John stared at his hands on the steering wheel. "I know."

Webb shut the door and watched the car pull away from the curb. He walked into his building and the metal door slammed behind him. As he climbed the stairs he saw Percy sitting at the top, holding a bottle. He smelled of urine and booze.

"Why don't you talk to me no more?"

Webb looked at the bottle and wondered if he could drink enough to erase a town's memory.

"I only told 'em what happened. They made me testify."

Webb stepped around Percy and went to his door. He stuck the key into the lock. Percy staggered to his feet.

"What did Earl want?" asked Percy.

"His sister," said Webb. He opened the door and let Percy inside.

Percy looked around the room. He took a sip from the bottle and handed it to Webb. Webb took a drink. He set the bottle on the table and peeled off his clothes. He hung his workpants on the shower rod and put on some underwear before taking another drink.

"You didn't invite me clamming yesterday," said Percy.

"I didn't go clamming. I haven't in twenty years."

Percy stared. There was no recollection in his eyes, just an old memory of a story he'd been practicing for two decades. Webb remembered when Percy had opinions, plans for the world, but now his eyes were hollow, lost in something invisible on the wall. Percy put out his hand for the bottle, but Webb shook his head.

"Gimme my goddamn bottle."

"No."

"See, I knew you never changed," said Percy. "You're a drunk like me."

Webb sat on his bed.

Percy lifted his shoulder and wiped his lips with the stump of his arm. He slid his back down the wall until he was sitting on the wooden floor.

"Percy. You need to take a bath."

"I clean myself."

"No, you don't. You gotta get in the water."

"I hate the water."

They sat in silence.

"So I stink?"

"It's not good," said Webb.

"We'll go clamming tomorrow."

Webb pulled himself off the bed. He lifted Percy up from

the floor and held him against the wall. "You gotta go."

"Make me a sandwich."

"Not tonight."

"You owe me a bottle."

Webb stretched his hands and balled them into fists. "I need you to go."

Percy stood at the door. "You never cared about me."

"I went to prison."

"You don't give a shit about no one." He opened the door and went into the hallway.

Webb shut the door. He turned out the light. He tilted the bottle to his lips and stared into the darkness. Another sip and the room turned gray. He could see the vague outline of the drawings on his wall. Another sip and a pale light crept into the room. He gazed at the black rock jutting into the surf.

He tore one of his drawings from the wall, put his fingers on either side and ripped it down the middle. And then he did it again, until a pile of small squares fell into the trash pail like confetti. He did it with each drawing, until there was no ocean, no rock, nothing to remind him of the past. He drank until there was no woman, no crime, just this room, these bare walls that pulled him close.

He tilted the bottle again, but it was dry.

He steadied himself, carried himself to the bathroom and unzipped his fly.

"Permission to use the head, sir?"

"Permission granted."

61

Alice woke up early and went into the bathroom. The shower curtain was gone and Ruth's makeup littered the counter. She knocked on Ruth's door.

"Get lost, Bellevue."

"I want to talk to you."

"Get in line."

"Where's the shower curtain?"

"How should I know?"

Alice banged again. "Hey," she said. "I'm sorry about yesterday, okay? I'm sorry I got upset with you."

"Why would you want to share some curtain with filth like me anyhow, *Bellview?*"

"Who said you were filth? Jesus. I'm apologizing. Would you please open the door?"

She heard Ruth roll off her mattress, and then the sound of scissors cutting plastic. A moment later the door opened. An arm reached out and handed Alice the bottom half of the shower curtain.

"What am I supposed to do with this?"

"Use it as a suppository, bitch."

"I said I was sorry."

"No wonder you got no friends. I don't know what I was thinking wasting my time with you."

A burly young mill worker stepped into the hall. "You can use my shower if you like."

"Thanks, I'm fine." She went to the bathroom and locked the door. She pushed the nozzle to the wall, then turned on the water and climbed in.

62

Webb broke boxes in the stock room. He crushed them hard under his boot, and when he heard the honk from George's truck he walked into the alley.

The old man limped to the rear, avoiding Webb's eyes. Webb lifted the parcels from the truck. He carried them inside and loaded them into the display case. George stood on the opposite side of the glass, waiting for Webb to smooth the ice. Webb crossed his arms and looked at the old man.

"Let's go," said George, but Webb didn't move.

The old man cleared his throat. He hobbled to the stock room and returned with a pair of gloves. He growled at Webb to get out of his way, then reached into the display case and smoothed the ice until it was flat. When he was done he pulled the gloves from his hands and smacked them one at a time against his thigh. "She was gonna find out anyway."

He walked back to the stock room.

Webb imagined the weight of a blade burying into the soft flesh of the crippled man's back. He watched George push open the flimsy door and glance over his shoulder before disappearing into the stock room.

Later, George told Webb to bring all the canned goods that lost their labels and stack them on a shelf with a discount sign. Webb dried each one individually and stacked them, a couple hundred identical silver cans in a pyramid formation.

At 10:30 a.m. George limped to the front of the store and Webb went outside for his break. Standing at the curb he gazed down at the river, swollen now and spilling onto the boardwalk. He strained for a glimpse of the Whitehorse Restaurant but all he could see were trees.

63

J ane Tripp looked up from her egg salad sandwich to see Webb standing in the doorway.

"They buzzed me in," he said.

The German Shepherd followed Webb with his eyes as he entered and sat across from Tripp.

Licking her fingers she asked if he knew why she had requested to see him during his lunch hour.

"Cause you heard about last night."

"What happened?"

He stared at his shoes. "I needed a drink."

"Do you think this is a joke, Mr. Cooley?" She studied him. "Because it isn't funny." She lifted a pickle from her lunch box and bit into it; the crunching echoed through the room.

"No, ma'am. I don't think it's funny," he said.

"Then tell me why you went there."

He thought for a moment. "I think I'm tired of people looking at me like I'm going to hurt them."

She stopped chewing. "Are you afraid you might hurt someone?"

He looked at the long row of windows across the upper wall.

"Mr. Cooley?"

"No."

"Why did Officer Smith find you walking out past the city limits?"

"I was trying to get to the ocean."

"Is that really where you were going? In the middle of the night?" she asked.

He looked up, realizing where she was leading him.

"It's my job to help you, Mr. Cooley. But when you behave like this it's difficult to be on your side." The dog sighed heavily. His tail slapped the floor. "Were you going to your father's house?"

"No."

"Do you think the board set these limits to punish you?"

"No, ma'am."

"Well then, why were you walking out past the city limits last night?"

"I just told you."

Tripp cleared her throat. She twisted the top off a bottle of soda and took a sip. "Mr. Cooley, are you aware that this is the kind of behavior that put you into prison in the first place?"

"I'm not trying to hurt anyone."

"What do you think I should tell the board?"

"Just what I told you."

She put a hand over her mouth to hide a burp. "That you were going to visit the ocean? That you're drinking and you're out walking past the city limits at midnight? Mr. Cooley, you clearly don't understand. You are in violation of your parole, and that's all you have to say?"

He stared out the window. His jaw was stiff, as if to speak would implicate him. He wanted another drink.

"I'm going to speak to the board." She glanced at her book. "I want to see you here Thursday morning, first thing. That means before work."

"Yes, ma'am."

"Please tell Mrs. Harding to give me ten minutes."

"Yes, ma'am."

64

Alice walked into Buffalo Burgers. The rear door was unlocked but the restaurant was silent. She walked into the kitchen. The room was dark, but a light glowed from under the doorway of the office. Alice was about to knock when she heard sniffling inside. She walked through to the waitress station and began wrapping forks and knives in napkins while staring at the aging black-and-white photograph on the wall of a group of men proudly holding the corpse of a marlin.

Jimmy emerged from the office wearing a bandage on his right wrist.

"You okay?" she asked. He shrugged.

"What happened," she asked.

"I cut myself."

"How?"

"Just a stupid accident."

*　*　*

At lunchtime Alice saw Lester sitting at a table by himself.

"Well, hello there." She removed her pad and pen. "What are you having?"

"To be honest, I already ate," he said. "Maybe I'll have some French fries, though I really just came to make sure we're on for tonight."

"But it's not a date, right?"

"Hell no. It's a barbecue."

"Give me your address."

*   *   *

After lunch, Alice stood next to Jimmy in the waitress station. She filled the ketchup bottles while he filled the saltshakers. "I hate this place," he said. "I know it all looks great to you, but it's not"

"What happened?"

"My father said I could take his car to the dance, then last night he changed his mind. He doesn't want me to go to college. He wants me to stay and run this goddamn stupid place."

"Did you get in a fight?"

"I called him a liar, and he hit me. So I went upstairs and punched a hole in my bedroom window."

"Oh no."

"He had to drive me to the hospital to get the glass out of my hand. I got blood all over his car, and now I have to tell Bethany I can't take her to the dance."

"Gosh, I'd let you use my car, but I'm meeting someone tonight."

Jimmy screwed the lid on a saltshaker. "Thanks, that's not why I was telling you. I appreciate it though."

"Well, maybe if you dropped me off and picked me up it

could work out."

"You don't have to do that."

"Jimmy, I want you to go this dance."

He couldn't look at her face. He reached for her elbow and gripped it tightly. Alice smiled and squeezed his arm.

65

Webb scraped gum from the floor. When he glanced up he saw three boys through the window, coming up the hill. They crossed the street and walked toward the store. The blond boy noticed Webb watching them and nudged his friend. A moment later, they entered. Webb could see George's silhouette behind the one-way mirror.

"Hello, Mr. Cooley," said the boy, smirking. His friends strode the aisles, shoving each other and making noises, while Webb waited for George to storm through the door screaming at him to grab them.

"You better leave."

"Why? You gonna kill us?"

The boys laughed. They pulled a metal shelf over and it crashed to the floor, sending candy bars sliding across the store. The boys ran to the door. The blond kid followed them. Webb glanced at George's perch to see his silhouette was gone. He braced himself.

After a minute he wondered if he mistook the silhouette

for something else. He busied himself tidying up the front of the store and spent the next hour waiting on customers. Every couple of minutes he glanced at the one-way mirror, but saw nothing. At four-thirty he rang up the sole customer in the store, and when she left he walked back and pushed open the stock room door to use the toilet.

It looked like George was resting on his back on the concrete floor. And then he saw the pool of brown blood under his head. His chair lay next to him with one of the legs broken, snapped in the middle and hanging by a splinter. Webb took his wrist and found a faint pulse. Putting his arms under the old man's knees and neck, he lifted him gently and pushed through the stock room door.

A woman screamed when she saw Webb moving toward her with George hanging limply in his arms.

"Is he okay?"

"He fell."

"Oh my God," she said. She reached for her cell phone. "I'll call the hospital."

Drops of blood the size of quarters fell from the gash in the old man's head, plopping onto the sidewalk as Webb climbed the hill. Heads turned. A car slowed and a man followed him with his eyes. Reaching the hill's crest, Webb headed west toward the Waiden Health Center.

"He fell," Webb explained to the nurse at the front desk.

Without taking her eyes from Webb, she told him to put George on the gurney against the wall. "Doctor Giles, we have an emergency," she said into the phone.

A moment later a doctor and an attendant strode down the hall wearing scrubs. The doctor glanced at George and signaled to the attendant to get him to the ER.

Webb sat in the waiting room when John Smith entered.

"Webb, what are you doing here?"

"You know what I'm doing here."

"No, I just heard George fell, that's all."

"That's what happened."

"Okay, Okay." John lifted his palms. "I didn't say anything."

John sat across from Webb who returned to his magazine. He couldn't think. He was scared. No one believed him. No one believed anything he said.

"So, what exactly happened?"

"He fell off his platform. I wasn't there. I was working."

"I'm not arguing with you, Webb. I just want to get the facts."

The doctor pushed open the door. He nodded to John. "Hey Webb, can I ask you, how far did he fall?"

"About six feet."

The doctor addressed John. "We did a CAT scan. He has a basal skull fracture." He ran a finger up the rear of his head. "He's unconscious, but there seems to be very little internal bleeding."

"Is he going to be okay?" asked John.

"We'll keep him off his Warfarin. We're giving him plasma to thicken the blood. I spoke to a surgeon in Portland. If there's any complications we can bring him up there."

John nodded.

Through the window, Webb watched two men in jogging shorts sprint effortlessly down the road, carrying on a conversation as they ran.

Webb stood up.

"Where you going?" asked John.

"Back to work."

John and the doctor looked at each other as Webb opened the door and walked outside.

66

Alice parked in the Frontier Hotel parking lot. She walked to the front door and saw Webb descending the hill. When he met her gaze she looked away. As he reached the door of the general store something made her stop. She walked toward him. He stood waiting, and she stopped a short distance away.

"There's something on your shirt," she said.

"It's blood," he said. "George fell in the stock room. Hit his head. I just brought him to the hospital."

Her eyes dropped to the trail of brown dime-sized spots dotting the sidewalk up the hill. "Is he okay?"

He cleared his throat. "He's unconscious."

She glanced again at the blood on the concrete. The sky darkened. It wasn't raining, but when a car drove past its tire hit a pothole and sent water spraying onto the sidewalk behind them. "I didn't do anything to him," he said.

"I know," she said.

He reached for the door.

"Wait."

He stopped.

She didn't know what to say, she only knew what she wanted to ask him. "I wish you'd told me," she said.

"You didn't want to know." He opened the door.

"Webb, wait."

"What," he said. "Would it have made a difference? You were never planning on staying. I'm sure this makes it real convenient for you."

A couple walked down the hill. Alice squeezed her arms together, hugged herself from the cold. "I'm just trying to understand. Don't act like there's something wrong with me for wanting to understand. Maybe I wasn't planning on staying. I don't even know. That's the truth. But don't make me the bad guy for wanting to hear what happened."

"You know what happened. You heard it. I'm not that person anymore. I'm trying real hard to be someone new." He opened the door.

"Webb."

"No," he said. "I can't do this."

"I'm not the one who's running away."

"You already did."

"You think I'm supposed to be all right with it?"

"You were never gonna stay. It would have been just fine for you if you'd never known."

"So I used you? Is that what you think?"

"No, I'm sure a part of me didn't want you to know either."

"Just because you're trapped here doesn't mean I am. The truth is I don't know if I was going to stay or not. I just don't."

"Is that true? You're using me to get over your husband."

"Okay. Yes! That is true. Or it was true. I don't know. I have feelings for you too, Webb."

"I have to get to work."

"Why? He's not even here. He's in the hospital. The guy treats you like shit. What do you care?"

"It's my job. Besides, there's nothing to talk about."

She squeezed her eyes shut. "I just told you how I feel. What do you want from me?"

He shook his head. "I want you to look at me like you did before you found out."

She reached for his hand. "Can we talk about it?"

He pulled his hand away. "You don't understand what you're asking."

He opened the door and went inside.

67

Alice pulled into Jimmy's driveway and kept the engine running. A figure emerged from the front door in blue tights and a Superman T-shirt. An orange beach towel trailed from his shoulders. He approached the car solemnly, his right arm in a sling.

She opened her door. "Why don't you drive?"

He climbed into the driver's seat and tried to reach the key with his uninjured hand. She turned the key for him, starting the car.

"Can you do this?" she asked.

"Once I got it in drive, I'll be all right. I just need you to shift for me." He stepped on the brake and she put it in reverse. "What do you think of my costume?"

"Oh, is that a costume?" she asked.

He grinned. "Put 'er in drive."

68

Webb lay on his bed in the dark. He could smell her scent on the sheets. When he took the pillow away, flashing lights played against the wall. Car doors slammed and a moment later heavy footsteps climbed the stairs. He heard muttering, and then a knock on the door. "Hey Webb, it's John. We need to talk to you."

"Give me a minute." He went to the bathroom and splashed water on his face. He opened the door and squinted out at John Smith and Randy Smart standing under the florescent lights in green uniforms.

Randy was enormous. His right hand hovered near his belt, his feet slightly apart. "You alone?"

Webb nodded. "Yeah, what's up?"

"We just wanted to ask you . . ." said John, but Randy cut him off.

"We need you to come with us."

Webb looked at John who nodded apologetically.

"I told you what happened."

"We need to ask you some questions."

"I carried him to the hospital."

"He's in a coma," said Randy.

A door opened across the hall. A man peeked out, and then went back inside.

"You can ask me here," said Webb.

John chewed on his lip. "Maybe you should just come with us."

"No." Webb shook his head. "I didn't do anything."

Randy smiled, a half-grin. John's shoulders slumped as he stepped forward. Webb tried to close the door, but Randy got between him and the doorframe.

"Randy, hold on," said John. "Webb, don't do this."

"Are you arresting me?"

"Damn right," said Randy. He had his cuffs out and was pushing on the door. "Here we go now," he said, snapping them open. "Chrissakes Smith, you gonna help me?"

John pressed Webb against the door, shoving his left arm behind his back.

They led him down the stairs. A crowd gathered outside the Pastime watching Webb being led to the car. Randy and John guided him into the back seat, then slammed the door. As Randy came around the driver's side, Webb watched him raise his hand and tilt his chin like he was saluting. He started the engine and did a slow U-turn, heading back down the hill past the crowd, the flashing lights bouncing off the windows. Webb kept his eyes low staring at the vinyl seat in front of him.

"Maybe you could turn off the light show," said John.

"Relax," said Randy. He crept past the crowd before reaching to the dashboard and killing the lights.

69

Jimmy pulled up to a small saltbox house on the corner. Before he had time to get out of the car, Bethany burst from the front door and walk-jogged toward them, wearing a blue and white gingham dress with red shoes. She saw Alice sitting in the passenger seat and she slowed, her expression changed. Alice got out and opened the back door. "Jimmy's going to drive me to a friend's house, and then you guys can take my car." Bethany nodded and climbed into the front seat. She reached over and held onto Jimmy's bandaged hand.

Jimmy drove out past the town's limits and pulled up to a driveway nearly hidden by trees. He turned in and the lane opened up to a wide well-tended lawn at the middle of a circular drive. "Holy shit," he said.

"Wow," said Bethany. "This dude's loaded."

A rock garden lay at the edge of a one-and-a-half- story stone and cedar house. A pair of antique sodium lamps lit the broad front porch. Alice said goodbye to Jimmy and Bethany and climbed out from the back seat. She walked toward the house and before she reached the porch, Jimmy drove away.

She rang the bell. A light went on in the hallway and Lester appeared, walking towards her in jeans and a denim shirt. He opened the door and glanced outside. "Where's your car?"

"I got dropped off. You have me till ten." She stood in the foyer, gazing into the sunken living room with mahogany floors.

"Uh oh. I'm only charming till nine-thirty."

"Let me call them back." She turned to leave.

He grabbed her elbow and she walked down the steps into the living room. Above the fireplace was an abstract lithograph.

"Is that a Diebenkorn?" she asked.

"How did you know that?"

She wanted to say that everyone in her world knows Richard Diebenkorn, but instead said, "I went to art school."

"I was in a gallery in San Francisco a couple of years ago. I'm not an art guy, but I'd never seen anything like it. Still don't know why I got it. It cost me a fortune, but I love it." He laughed. "You're the first one who hasn't made fun of me for buying it."

She cocked her head. "So, is this whole hick cowboy routine just an act to keep the locals from kicking your ass?"

He grinned. "Pretty much. You want a beer or should I open some red wine?"

"Wine is good."

In the kitchen he poured two glasses of wine. He held one up for her. "Happy Halloween."

He led her out to a back deck where a small fire crackled in a pit. In the corner, steam rose from a hot tub. Alice stood at the veranda and gazed down hundreds of feet to the river. "This is the Yaquina?"

"Sometimes, in the morning, the mist comes right up

to the deck. It feels like you could step off and walk into the clouds. In the spring, when the sun sets, the river turns purple."

Alice sat on a deck chair next to the fire. She looked up through the canopy of overhanging trees into the starlit night. He wiped the dust off the chair next to her and sat down. The lights from a jetliner blinked in the distance as it inched across the night sky.

"Does your ex-wife still live around here?"

"Erin? Yeah, she works in town at the bank. You've probably seen her, dark hair, sort of innocent-looking, but deep down she's the devil."

"Are you still friends?"

"Not exactly. We're civil."

"But no kids, right?"

"No. Thank God."

Alice sipped her wine.

"Is that it?" he asked. "Are those all the questions?"

"For now."

"You know, there's something to be said for getting the sex out of the way, so we can relax and focus on getting to know each other."

"Don't do that," she said.

"Sorry. I'm nervous."

"It's okay," she said. "Do you ever miss her?"

"Erin?" He gazed at the stars and laughed. "No. Not even a little."

"What happened with the other one?"

"Gloria is still a mystery. I think her mother got into her head, told her how things ought to be. It should have worked. I don't know. Maybe it wasn't meant to be. Isn't that the answer to everything these days? Chalk it up to fate so no one has to feel guilty."

"Or change," she said.

"Right."

He took a long sip of wine. He reached across and took her hand. She let it linger for a moment, and then pulled it away.

The deck was silent. A wolf howled in the distance. She took another sip of wine and closed her eyes. "It's so peaceful."

"Sometimes I think it's a curse. I inherited the place from my folks and I've never wanted to give it up. I almost sold it after Erin. I was going to sell everything and just move to San Francisco or Portland, and work my way up the ladder."

"Why didn't you?"

"Ah, I'm sure there's a good psychological explanation. Maybe I'm just lazy."

"You're definitely not lazy."

"Everyone gave me a million reasons not to go. San Francisco's expensive. All your people are here. You'll turn gay. I guess they wore me down."

"Do you regret it?"

He looked into the darkness. "Sometimes. But then I think, I got this great life, why the hell do I want more?"

She got up and went to the veranda, stared down through the treetops to the river winding silently through the canyon. "I can see why you wouldn't want to leave."

He smiled wanly. "Yeah, well . . ."

"What?"

"Nothing, just . . ." he sighed deeply. "It's a mill town."

"What does that mean?"

"They've been closing down consistently since the eighties when the environmentalists started making a fuss. Nobody replanted back then, and so the government tightened its grip on federal land. Now we're reaping what we didn't sow. AFP has its own land, two thousand acres, but when that's cut the party's over."

"How long will that last?"

"Cy Fischer told me five more years. He owns the mill. They haven't won a government contract in seven years. He's not even bothering to replant. Says it'll be another fifty years before anyone could cut again."

"What'll happen to the town?"

"Yup. Exactly. That's the big question. Some folks'll retire, and maybe there'll be enough business to sustain downtown. Every place is different. Some towns limp by for a while, others just shut down."

"What about you?"

He looked at his barbecue. "I keep hoping something's gonna change. You'd think after seeing this happen for thirty years, we'd all get it. I don't know what it is. Something keeps you from thinking it's actually going to happen here."

"Nobody talks about it?"

"Right," he said. "We're all thinking, 'Well, nobody's leaving, why should I?'" He stared at her. "I look at you, and I start thinking how it would make it all . . ."

"What?" she said. "Bearable?"

"No. I was going to say . . . I just feel like if I had a reason to go out there, something more than myself, I could really dig in, work those eighty-hour weeks. A man needs something to come home to."

He looked up at the stars.

"I wish I didn't just say that," he said.

"Me too."

"That was stupid."

"A little premature."

"I'm going to put those burgers on."

He went inside. She sat and wondered if she had just been

proposed to.

He returned with four burger patties on a plate. "Can we pretend I didn't just say that?"

"Say what?"

He put the patties on the grill. "It's not even a date for God's sake."

"It's okay, I understand. It's scary to make a change like that."

"Thanks."

The doorbell rang.

"Who the hell is that?" he said. "Hold on."

He went back inside, and this time closed the sliding door behind him. Alice sat and stared out into the darkness, and then she heard the sound of a woman laughing. She opened the door and walked through the kitchen to the hall where she stood watching Lester at the front door.

Over his shoulder, she saw a pretty young blonde woman standing on the porch. Next to her was a small child wearing a white sheet over its head with two holes cut out for the eyes.

"What kind of excuse is that," said the woman. Alice could hear the playfulness in her voice. "We came all this way, and we don't get any candy?"

Alice froze. She suddenly felt like she was intruding.

She was about to turn back when the woman saw her, and Lester spun around. "Oh, hey, Gwen, this is my friend, Alice. Alice, this is my neighbor, Gwen."

Gwen's eyes darted to Lester, wounded, as Alice walked toward them.

"Hi, I'm the *neighbor*," said Gwen, with a bite in her voice. "I'm sorry, Lester, I didn't realize you had a date."

"It's not a date," said Alice. "We're just friends."

"Hey, no, it's . . ." Gwen fidgeted with her earring.

"Anyway, we should get going."

Lester's face flashed panic, and then he smiled. "This is Gwen's son, Evan. I mean, Spooky. Right?"

The boy was silent. He reached for his mother's hand while Gwen quickly looked Alice up and down.

"We were just trying to think of what I could give Evan," said Lester. "I wasn't expecting any trick or treaters."

"That's all right," said Gwen. She pulled her son's hand. "We were just driving past."

"Are you sure?"

"Mama, I want some candy."

"He doesn't have any. Come on, let's go, Evan." She dragged the kid across the porch and down the steps.

Alice watched her open her truck door and shove the boy inside. She climbed into the driver's side and drove around the grass island, sending gravel flying as she peeled out of the driveway.

"She seems nice," said Alice. "Too bad we didn't have any candy."

Lester looked at her. His smile faded. "What? Go ahead."

Alice shrugged. "It's none of my business."

"You want to ask me, so go ahead."

"That was a wedding ring on her finger, wasn't it?"

He scratched the back of his head. "You asked if I missed my ex-wife. I do. To be honest, yes, sometimes a lot, and so . . ." He didn't finish his sentence. Instead he started a new one. "I'm not sure why, cause we sure didn't get along very well."

Alice looked into his eyes and listened. He mumbled something about dinner, and she watched him walk back to the kitchen. She followed him out to the deck where he stood in front of the barbecue staring into the grill. Smoke billowed from the charring meat.

"They're burning," she said.

"I barely know her husband," he said. He flipped the meat onto a plate and went inside. She stood on the deck, and after a couple of minutes she went inside.

He stood in the kitchen staring into the refrigerator.

"What are you doing?"

"Trying to find something for us to eat."

"We could order out."

"There's no delivery service in Waiden." He closed the fridge door. "Fuck," he muttered under his breath.

"It's okay," she said.

"You're working as a waitress," he said. "Your last boyfriend killed his wife. I was kinda hoping you'd consider me a step up."

Alice became aware of the hum of the refrigerator and the ticking of the clock on the wall. "I should probably go home," she said.

"I thought this was going to be fun," he said.

"Me too."

70

Webb lay on the metal bunk, hands behind his head, staring at the wire mesh supporting the mattress above him. Paul Childers lay on the cold cement floor in a thin acrylic sweater, his body twisted awkwardly. He grunted, awakening from a drunk, his eyes straining to make his bearings. He touched the dried blood under his nose and winced. "Goddamn it." He closed his eyes.

Webb shifted on his cot and Paul's eyes blinked open. He sat up like an animal. He looked at Webb and his face broke into a delirious grin. He licked gingerly at a loose tooth. "Hey Webb, look at us."

Webb went back to staring at the mesh.

"My mouth feels like a frog took a shit in it," said Paul.

Webb rolled off the mattress. He ran water from the metal sink into a Styrofoam cup and handed it to Paul. Paul sat up and took small sips but the water dribbled down his chin.

"How's your brother?" asked Webb.

"Who? LJ?"

"You got another one?"

Paul stared.

Webb sighed. "How's LJ?"

"LJ's dead. He drank bleach."

"On purpose?"

"I reckon so. He left a note said it was no one's fault. I know momma appreciated that."

"When?"

Paul massaged his temple. His fingers were yellow. "Maybe ten years ago. Son of a bitch thought he was Jesus."

"Is that why he killed himself?"

"No, he liked that. It was when he realized he wasn't that things went downhill." Paul tilted the last of the water into his mouth and gargled. He spat against the wall. "He was with Shane and Percy and them. They got into the meth. LJ got so scabby momma didn't recognize him. Now the burden's on me."

Webb closed his eyes. After a minute he felt hot air on his face. He opened his eyes. Bloodshot pupils stared at him from inches away.

"I heard 'em talking," he said, gesturing down the hall. "That boss of yours is in the hospital." His lips were cracked. His breath was terrible. "I got some ideas."

"Close your mouth."

"Why? They can't hear me."

"No, I can smell you."

Paul retreated, backing up on all fours. "I was thinking, we sneak over to his house while he's still in the hospital. See what we can find." He wiped his mouth with a dirty palm. "What's the matter, you deaf?"

Webb shook his head.

"Who's gonna know?" he asked. "You're staring at me.

You're giving me the heebies," he said. "All right, maybe I'll go myself."

"He's got a dog that'll kill you."

"I ain't scared of no mutt."

"And if *it* don't . . ."

"What? You will?" He laughed. "What about honor among thieves?"

"I'm not a thief."

Paul went back to the corner and lay on his back. He groaned and covered his eyes with his arm.

Later, John pushed the key into the lock and slid open the door. "Hospital called, said he came to a half hour ago. Says he fell."

Webb stood up and walked past him.

"Hey, Webb." Paul sat in the corner, his body twisted toward the wall. "You weren't serious, were you?" Webb nodded, and Paul's face broke into a grin. "Don't worry, Mac, I'll be good." Webb walked down the hall next to John. "I ain't no thief *either*," cried Paul. "I got prospects."

Webb walked through the office. Randy Smart sat hunched over his desk typing something onto an old computer. Webb walked silently past him and out into the night.

71

Lester kept his eyes on the road while Alice stared out the passenger window. He pulled up to the curb outside the hotel.

"Thanks." She reached for the door handle. "You think I'm an asshole," he said.

"No, I don't." She let go of the door handle. "I really don't."

He looked across the street at the Pastime. "We're all just sitting in there waiting for something to happen."

He leaned over and kissed her cheek, but she pressed a hand to his chest.

"I don't think that's gonna make either of us feel better."

"I'm sorry," he said.

"That's okay," she said. "Goodnight." She climbed out of the car.

He pulled away.

She stared across the street. Webb sat at the counter inside Corky's. She crossed the street and entered. Her face was hot as she sat on the stool next to his.

He put a French fry into his mouth. "How was your date?"

She looked out at the street and then at the waitress. "Could I get a side of fries?"

"Here." He pushed his plate toward her.

"Just a cup of tea then." Alice took a fry and dipped it into the ketchup. "How's George?"

"He's awake."

"Is he badly hurt?"

"Skull fracture." He watched her from the corner of his eye. He set his fork down. The waitress placed a cup of hot water and a tea bag in front of her.

"Why'd you come to me that first night?" he asked.

She gazed into the back kitchen. A man with a shaved head stared into the fryer.

"Is it just cause you didn't want to be alone?"

A pair of teenage girls sat in the corner eating fish sticks. One of them had her hair dyed black and wore fishnets and combat boots.

"I don't know. I thought it was, but I'm not sure now."

"I wish you hadn't," he said.

"I'm sorry."

"That's not why I said it."

"I know."

He put another forkful into his mouth. Through the window she watched Jimmy park her car outside the Frontier. He stepped from the driver's side and went into the hotel.

"I gotta go," she said. They sat quietly for a moment. She tore open the paper and placed the teabag into the cup.

He glanced around the restaurant. "My lawyer told the judge it was a crime of passion. Like I'd never thought of it before." He shook his head, like he was trying to shake off a memory. "But I had." He ate another fry. "I don't mean . . ."

he swallowed. "I just mean sometimes I couldn't see choices. Everything just kept getting louder and I didn't know how to turn down the volume. The prosecutor called me a monster. I woulda done anything for her," he said. "Instead I did that."

"You're a different person now, right?"

"I don't know." He shrugged. "I want to say I am, but I honestly don't know. What if I'm not?"

"You have to forgive yourself."

"Why? Why do I have to do that?"

"Because no one else is going to. Can I ask you something? If George was unconscious, how did you get him to the hospital?

Webb cleared his throat. "I carried him."

"You're kidding?"

"Why?"

Alice smiled. "Cause *I* wanted to kill him, and he didn't do anything to me."

"He's just miserable. It's not personal."

For a while they sat in silence. "When I think about what happened . . . I just . . ." Webb hesitated. "I can't get enough distance to see what it really was. How do you know you're never going to do something like that again?"

"We have to have faith."

He chuckled. "I thought you didn't believe in God."

"I don't. I just mean something bigger than how scared we are."

"Maybe some folk are meant to be alone."

"Are you?" she asked.

"Probably."

"Then why'd you buy a table with two chairs?"

He looked at her.

"Webb, I don't know what happened. But I'm not afraid

of you."

He stared into his plate of French fries. She watched him breathing, turning it over in his mind like a riddle he couldn't untangle, searching for an answer that would bring it all around, until the words bubbled to the surface. "Well, I'm afraid of *you*," he said.

Jimmy watched her from outside the Frontier.

"I better go."

She stood and went to the door.

"Hey," he said. "That wasn't true, what I said."

"About what?"

"Wishin' you didn't come over that first night."

"I'm glad. See ya."

She walked out to her car.

72

Jimmy handed her the keys. He sat in the passenger seat in his homemade Superman costume, his knees pressed neatly together.

"Where's Bethany?"

"She got a ride home with Brad Stonesifer."

Alice started the car and pulled away from the curb. Across the street, she noticed Lester's car parked up the hill from the Pastime. "Who the hell is Brad Stonesifer?"

"Just some asshole," said Jimmy. "I was sitting with her and then Brad asked her to dance. I thought she was going to say no, but he made her laugh. He was dressed up as a bald guy in a suit, and he made some stupid joke and she started laughing. And when the song ended, she stayed on the dance floor. I think she's his girlfriend now."

"Oh Jimmy, I'm sorry."

"I went to the cafeteria to get some potato chips and when I went back to the gym, they were gone. I went outside and they were holding hands."

"What a tacky bitch."

"So I just sat in your car all night until it was time to come and pick you up, but when I got there, the house was empty and I didn't know if maybe Mr. Heffelfinger was already giving you a ride home."

"Jimmy, I know it hurts, but . . ."

"No, I shoulda done something. I'm a puss."

"You did the right thing. Screw 'em. They deserve each other."

As she drove, she glanced over to see Jimmy staring out the window. "You're a great guy," she said. "Any girl'd be lucky to have you."

When she pulled up to his house, she parked in the driveway. A light went on, and Jimmy's father stood at the window.

"It's not even real buffalo meat," said Jimmy. "The buffalo farm went out of business but he didn't want to have to buy a new sign, so now we just put oregano in regular beef."

"Well," said Alice, "you'd never know it."

"Anyway." Jimmy opened the door. "I'm not supposed to tell you this, it's supposed to be a surprise, but tomorrow you're our employee of the month."

Alice smiled. "Jimmy, I'm just very fond of you." She leaned over and took his hand. She pulled him to her and kissed him on the cheek.

He shut the door and she watched the figure in the cape walk into the night. The charcoal mist blurred the edges of Jimmy, until she could no longer distinguish where he ended and the night began. She watched the upstairs bedroom light blink on. He tore the cape from his collar and threw it onto the bed.

She put her car into gear and drove with the window

down. The cold air numbed her face, but she liked the rush of wind past her ears. It kept her company. As she drove an overwhelming sense of loneliness pressed in on her. There was a rising panic in her chest and her mind searched for someone to connect with, someone to distract her from this feeling — but there was no one left. In one way or another she had distanced herself from everyone in her life.

She put her foot on the brake and pulled to the side of the road. She climbed out of the car and stared at the dark, starless night. Her breath was short and quick. Her mind raced, searching for an escape, but then she stopped. She planted her feet and waited. This rotten dread clawed in her chest, but she didn't move. She waited to be swallowed into the abyss. She waited for the universe to deliver the terrible news. And as she waited, she felt something wrench inside her, like something was unlocking and she could breathe. "I'm not alone," she whispered.

Was it an accident, she thought, that she had ended up in Waiden? Her life with Chick was so filled with distraction that she wondered if she had done it on purpose, all the way down to destroying her cell phone.

It wasn't Chick that had prevented her from pursuing a creative life — it was her fear of being alone. But what was she afraid to discover that had kept her so active, her mind calculating each move, until, exhausted, she had made the choice to lose herself in someone who offered her a prefabricated life? She knew the moment she met Chick that he was wrong for her, and also that she would marry him. Something electric passed between them, a jolt that jangled her brain, but she embraced the fear, kidding herself it was something she must conquer rather than a choice she was making to escape herself. She would have done anything for him, the way a hostage would for her captor. She was an accessory, and had always known it, but she'd convinced herself otherwise to avoid the truth that she'd chosen him. And yet, she'd had this epiphany a thousand times before, but after sitting, post-breakfast, with Chick, and staring out the window of their sprawling penthouse condo together discussing whether to summer in Bali or rent a chateau in Normandy, her resolve invariably weakened.

After all, she had won. Chick was her trophy. She had arrived and the hors d'oeuvres were outstanding. She was the focal point, the blonde goddess wife of rock royalty who was not about to surrender her station simply because she was miserable. To leave meant spoiling the illusion she had spent years constructing. Alice wasn't afraid of her marriage collapsing, but of exposing the lie she had built.

She parked her car in the parking lot of the Frontier Hotel and walked inside. She handed Milo five dollars and asked for change in quarters.

Picking up the payphone, she jammed in the quarters and dialed Chick's number.

"Hello?"

"Chick, it's me."

There was silence on the other line. And then, "What do you want?"

"I just wanted to say I'm sorry."

"Uh huh," he said. "Where are you?"

"Oregon," she said, "in some shitty hotel."

"Why?" he asked.

"Why?"

"What the fuck are you doing there?"

"Waitressing."

"You must really hate me."

"I don't. And I'm sorry I bolted like that."

"Why did you?" he asked.

"Fear," she said.

"How 'bout elaborating?"

She stared at the beige paint peeling off the ceiling and noticed that it was falling in small flakes onto the carpet. "I don't know how articulate I'll be," she said. "Just that I needed to be alone, and I was afraid I'd lose myself in you again."

"Again? Was I present when we previously discussed the etiology of this affliction?"

"Chick, I'm tired," she said. "I'm gonna have to mull that one over." She realized that she could have pursued her dreams with Chick, but then if she had, she would never have chosen him. All of the goals she sought in her early twenties, the ones she failed to accomplish by losing herself in him — there was no other way it could have gone. "I don't know if I can explain it any better," she said. "Just that I wish I could have done it more gracefully, and I'm sorry, I really am."

"So, you're not coming back," he said. She could hear the pain in his voice, and she realized how much she meant to him.

"No."

"You met someone, didn't you?"

"That's not why I left."

"But you did, didn't you?"

"I don't know. Yes. I think so."

He said nothing. He sighed.

She didn't want to hurt him, but there was something about his sigh that made her realize she had an effect on him. "And what about you?" she said.

"I'm fifty-six," he said. "I'm not Elizabeth Taylor. I'm not getting married a fourth time. It's not a sport."

He was telling her that she mattered to him, and it surprised her that she'd ever thought otherwise.

"Go do your thing," he said. She could hear the walls going up. He was never indifferent. He was just scared. "You always blamed me," he said. "Every one of you. I don't know what you wanted."

"You," she said.

"Again," he said. "No fucking idea what you're talking about."

She could hear the rage and despair in his voice. And then she heard the dial tone.

It was a parting shot, and maybe she deserved it. Her cheeks were wet when she hung up. As much as she had believed he was the problem, she had never investigated why she chose him.

She thought about Webb. Whatever fear she had of him was really a fear that she would not be able to leave. Yet, she wanted to be near him. But if she knocked on his door, was she just running away from herself again? She didn't know.

73

She entered Webb's building and climbed the stairs. She knocked. He opened the door and put his arms around her, pulling her into him, squeezing her tightly.

They lay together in the darkness, holding onto each other.

In the morning, he sat at his desk, putting on his shoes.

"Where are you going?"

"Work."

He stood up and went to the door. He said, "I want to take you to the Whitehorse tonight."

74

Webb threw George's broken chair into the trash bin in the back alley. He climbed the stairs to George's desk and opened the drawer where he found a ring of keys. He pulled down the gloves hanging from the nail and shoved them in his jacket pocket.

Walking along the side of the road, he headed inland. The cold air numbed his face. After three miles, he came to a mailbox that read G. Plotki. He walked up the lane to George's house, an old Craftsman with a long porch, set back from the road. He kicked through a yard of wet leaves and when he pushed the key into the front door, the barrel-chested beast with the thick ugly head and bloodshot eyes threw herself at the door. She lifted her paws to the window and barked and bared her teeth. Webb cursed. He cracked open the door and tossed the gloves inside. Pearl sniffed at them for a moment, then growled and rammed her head through the gap, snapping ferociously as Webb tried to pull it shut. He closed the door on her snout, and she yelped and wiggled away. She sniffed the gloves and made a whining sound.

"Your daddy's in the hospital," said Webb through the glass. He opened the door again and let her shove her fat head through the crack until he couldn't contain her. He stepped back and let her sniff him, then she bounded into the yard where she squatted and took a shit next to a tree.

"Atta girl."

Pearl looked at Webb. Cold eyes glowered. The bowlegged bitch sprinted, teeth bared in furious anger. Webb leapt inside the door, slammed it behind him as the animal crashed against it.

Webb walked through the house to the kitchen. On the floor next to the fridge was Pearl's bowl, licked clean. The water bowl was empty. He filled it from the tap and after a search, found a bag of dry dog food in the laundry room. He filled the bowl and went to the front door.

The dog raced back and forth in front of the house, trying to find a way in, embarrassed that her biological urge had trumped her duty. He opened the door slightly and she rammed her head against it, trying to smash her way inside. Webb shut the door, and she howled.

"It's okay."

He opened the door and held out the bowl, placed it outside. She ate, ravenous, her powerful jaw crunching hard, tossing her head in savage gulps.

He walked into the living room: hardwood floors, hook rugs, quilts and Shaker chairs. He gazed at the photographs, dozens of small pictures neatly framed and lined carefully along the mantle—pictures of a young man next to a pretty woman with auburn hair and a fierce smile. He stopped at one of the photographs. It was old, drained of color, a shot of the couple standing together in a garden surrounded by other couples, fellow tourists smiling for the camera. The woman's eyes were mischievous. The man looked thrilled and terrified next to her. Webb barely recognized George with his thick, dark hair and unlined face. There was something else, too, a life in his eyes, wonder at this small woman beside him. They were a part of it all; we are here, they were saying, like they could not believe their luck.

Webb wondered how often George stared at this photograph. He wondered if the old man relived these times, if he believed he could bring her back for a moment to remind him of why he was here. He went into the bedroom.

Her vanity stood in the corner of the room, the makeup kit and lipstick still on the table. She was alive to the old man, forever in the next room. He opened the closet. On one side was a rack of women's clothes, preserved in plastic, like he was anticipating her return.

Webb stopped in the living room and grabbed the black and white photograph of George and his wife and slipped it into his pocket.

The dog stood outside the front door, growling. He grabbed a chair and opened the door. She lunged at him, but he held the chair in front of him as they traded places and he stepped back outside.

75

Webb sat in the hospital waiting room. When the nurse appeared, he explained why he was there. "Oh," she said. "I'll be right back."

He pretended to read a magazine until the door opened and the doctor appeared.

"I need to speak to my boss," said Webb.

"He's sleeping right now. If you want to wait till he wakes up . . ."

Webb waited.

Twenty minutes later the nurse appeared and led him to George's room.

Webb stood at the door. George sat propped up with a tube in his nose and another in his arm. He looked at Webb through weary eyes.

"We're almost out of fish," said Webb.

"Get some more."

Webb shifted on his feet. "I can't leave town." He looked at his hands, working them, trying to get some feeling.

"You're useless. Worse than that."

Webb pushed his shoulder away from the doorframe and entered the room. "What?"

"Useless worm."

Webb looked down at the broken old man. He wanted to hit him, pull him from his bed and throw him across the room, smash his head through the wall, crush his skull under his boot, but when he looked into his eyes he saw the fear. He was tired, fed up; he wanted to be done. Webb reached down and touched the blanket, patted the old man's foot. He left his hand there. "I hope you feel better," he said.

Something in George's eyes shifted. The old man tried to scowl, but he was crying. Webb took his hand off the blanket and walked to the door.

There was a noise, a grunt. "Why didn't you leave me?" asked George.

Webb looked at George's hollow eyes, the soft folds of aging flesh fell from his cheeks, and suddenly he wondered if George had fallen on purpose, or at least partially on purpose, if he wanted to die.

"Wanted to make sure I got paid."

A thin smile crossed George's face. He made a choking sound and a clear line of drool ran down his chin. Webb took a tissue from the counter and wiped it away. He balled the tissue and tossed it in the basket. George whispered something, and then tried to pull the tube from his nose. Webb held him down.

"We need some help here."

A male orderly rushed in. He moved to the other side of the bed and lifted a couple of straps across George's body. George cursed them both. A nurse came in with a needle.

"He's hallucinating," said the orderly.

Webb and the orderly held him down while the nurse

tapped his arm for a vein.

"No!" George bucked.

"Relax, sir. This'll make you feel better."

"I got a dog."

"What did he say?"

"Said he got a dog."

The nurse scowled. "Is someone looking after his animal?" She pointed the needle at the ceiling. "You need someone to feed your dog, Mr. Plotki?"

George nodded.

"Does he bite?"

His eyes leaked a creamy liquid. "Course she bites."

Webb reached into his pocket and pulled out the framed photograph of George standing next to his bride. He placed it on the bedside table. "I just fed her," he said.

George glanced at the picture and blinked.

"I'm going to work," said Webb.

The nurse and the orderly watched Webb walk to the door.

"So, he fed her," said the orderly. "The man's taking care of it."

Webb walked down the hall and out to the street.

76

After the lunch rush, the restaurant emptied quickly. The mill workers rose as one, leaving a few bewildered travelers wondering if they missed a call to evacuate. Once the wait staff cleared the tables Jimmy ordered everyone to the front of the restaurant where he stood with a plaque and a handwritten speech. He told them that it gave him great pleasure to announce November's employee of the month. Everyone clapped as Jimmy recited a list of traits that aided Alice in winning the prize. He handed her the plaque and invited her to say a few words. She thanked everyone for making her feel welcome and expressed her excitement at continuing to be a part of the Buffalo Burgers team. The staff, along with an old couple from Vancouver applauded her.

77

Mrs. Packer shook out her umbrella and shuffled down the aisle with her basket. When she reached the back of the store, she peeked through the space between the floppy metal doors. She stood for a moment, then looked at Webb and pinched her lips together. She shook her head and returned her items to the shelves. She snapped open her umbrella, pushed on the door, and marched into the rain.

Later that morning, the kid entered with his pair of buddies. He caught Webb's look and marched brazenly up the aisle. "How are you today, Webb Cooley?"

"You planning on buying something?"

"Why? It ain't like we killed nobody."

"You better leave."

"Where's the old retard?" The kid dropped his mouth on the right side.

"What's your name?"

"What's it to you?"

"If I catch you stealin' again . . ."

The kid stuck out his chin. "What makes you think I'd take this junk?"

The other boys walked toward the door. The bigger one spoke from the corner of his mouth. "Trev, come on."

"So long, killer."

Webb lunged and the blond kid ran to the door. He pulled the door open and bolted outside.

Webb followed him. The kid tore up the hill, arms pumping, he flew past his comrades. The boys looked back to see Webb sprinting after them. The smallest one turned, stopped cold, arms raised to cover his head as Webb sprinted past him. The blond kid looked over his shoulder to see Webb approaching. His sneer turned to terror as Webb raced past the second boy. Candy bars fell from inside his jacket as he ran.

"Leave me alone." The blond kid stopped on the sidewalk.

Webb ignored him, pinned him against the wall. "Help!" shouted the kid. "Help!"

Down the street some folks turned to watch. Webb stepped back. "Open your pockets."

"Go to hell."

The front door of the hardware store opened. A man stepped out in a white apron. "What's the problem?"

"He's stealing from us," said Webb.

The man looked at the two boys watching from the bottom of the hill, then back at the kid. "Don't take shit from him, Webb." He went back inside.

Webb asked, "What's in those pockets?"

"None of your business."

"Empty 'em." He held him by the collar against the stone wall. "You want to go to the police?" He reached into the kid's jacket and pulled out a fistful of candy bars. The kid tried to run, but Webb grabbed him. "You want to go to juvie?"

"I don't care."

Webb clamped a hand on his arm and dragged him down the hill. "My old man's gonna kill you," he said. "They can't do nothin' . . . coupla candy bars."

"Lot more than that."

"Prove it."

"Don't have to. I'll just ask your buddies down there," he said, pointing at the two faces peeking from behind the bank.

"They ain't gonna snitch."

Webb told him to pick up the candy bars on the sidewalk. The kid did what he was told, and when he looked up, Webb saw he was going to cry.

"How you gonna make it up?"

"I didn't do nothin.'"

"All right, let's go to the police."

"Wait."

"What?"

"I could work for you."

"How many candy bars you figure you took? Coupla hundred?"

"Maybe."

"I figure an hour for every bar."

"That's bullshit."

"No, it's not, it's jail pay. Why aren't you in school?"

"We ditched."

"All right, I'll see you Saturday morning. And if you're not here by six a.m., I'll send the police after you."

Webb walked back to the store. He turned to see the kid walking backwards uphill. The kid sneered. He raised a middle finger and spat a stream of liquid from between his teeth.

78

It was dark when Alice pulled up to Jimmy's house. Jimmy sat in the passenger seat, balancing the box of receipts on his lap. "I need to talk to you," he said, his knee chattering.

She turned the headlights off and left the engine running with the heater on. "Are you okay?"

"I talked to Bethany this morning and . . ."

"Really? You talked to her?"

"I called her. She wants to get back together."

"Gosh. Okay," she said. "That's terrific, right?"

"Except she sort of feels like, kind of uncomfortable with us working together."

"Why?"

"It's not that she doesn't like you . . ."

"Why would she not like me?"

"I think she's intimidated."

"Is that why she went off with Brad Stonesifer?"

"That's what she said."

"Is there something I can do to help?"

"No. I don't think so." He stared down at the box. "I don't know. I mean, I told her nothing's going on between us."

"Oh. Did she think there was?"

"No. I don't know. Maybe."

"Why did she think that?"

"She's insecure. She said she was afraid of losing me."

"Well, good. You're a great guy."

"Thanks. And that's what I told her you said last night."

"What did I say?"

"Just that, you know, you think I'm a great guy, and that you're fond of me and all."

"Oh . . . well . . . I did say I was fond of you. Yes, but . . ."

"And I told her nothing's going on . . ."

"But why would you tell her that?"

He shrugged. "Cause it's true."

"Did she ask?"

He scratched his side. "No."

"Wait . . . so, you told her I said I was fond of you?"

His leg jiggled. "And I told her nothing's going on."

"But nothing *is* going on!"

"*I know.*"

"But when you say nothing is going on, it sometimes means something is going on. It's like planting a seed. You were trying to make her jealous."

"I don't know. Maybe I was. Anyway, I just think it might be better if you got a job somewhere else."

"What?!"

"I don't think this is working out."

"Are you joking?"

"No."

"You're firing me? You can't fire me."

He stared out the window.

Alice glanced up at the stars.

"She asked you to do this, didn't she? You're playing games with each other."

"We're in love."

"No, you're not, trust me. Your hormones are raging. You can't fire me just because she asked you to."

"I'm the manager."

"I'm employee of the month! How can you fire your employee of the month?!"

"We almost always give it to the newest person. It doesn't really mean anything." He opened the car door and climbed out. "I'll get Bethany to drive me home from now on. Sorry about this, Alice. I thought you were a really good waitress."

79

She didn't watch him walk to the house. The car door closed and she floored it. She passed the trailer park on her right. Ahead, a small sign with peeling paint read: MISTY'S ONE MILE. She slowed and turned at the stop sign. She drove down a bumpy gravel road for half a mile and pulled into the parking lot of a low one-story cinderblock building set back from the road. Half a dozen vehicles, mostly pickups, filled the lot.

She pushed open the door. The room stank of sweat and cigarettes. It was too hot, like a violent fever. A thin man with a doughy face and narrow, wide-set eyes stopped her. "Can I help you, lady?"

"You're Ricky, right?"

"Maybe," he said. "Who are you?"

"A friend of Ruth's."

A strange look registered on his face, like he'd been caught at something. He motioned with his head for her to enter. She stood in the shadows. A half dozen men sat in the dark watching something she couldn't see, their eyes set grimly toward the corner of the room. The room was quiet, ambient music crackled at low volume. Their faces were slack, lifeless, their hands gripped their drinks like IV drips, cigarettes sprouted from between their fingers.

Ricky watched her. She wanted to run, but she stepped further inside, peeking her head around the corner to see Ruth barefoot on a small plywood stage. An amber light made her look distant and unreal. She stared into the darkness. She did a slow shuffle. She held a breast and rubbed the nipple between her fingers.

A man said, "Christ, you're ugly. Like a goddamn horse."

"Screw you, Ted," said Ruth.

A man said, "When do we get a new one, Ricky?"

"Next week," said another. "This piggy goes home."

"You'll miss me when I'm gone," she said.

"Like I miss cancer," said Ted.

"I wish you died," said Ruth.

A man had a newspaper on his table. He tore off a strip, crumpled it and snapped it at Ruth, hitting her on the head.

She said, "There better be a dollar bill in there, Smitty."

Smitty didn't even grin. He reached for his beer and took a long angry gulp.

Alice turned. Ricky stared at her. She started to leave but he put his hand out. "Where you goin'?"

"What?"

"Stay here." He stood in front of her. "You wanna go up next?"

She shoved past him.

She ran to her car. Her heart slammed in her chest. She climbed inside and started the engine, threw the car into gear, and backed out of the parking lot. Her car bounced off the bumps as she fought her way back to the main road.

80

George's truck lurched forward. Webb came off the clutch. He looked in his rearview to see Pearl gulp her dinner in the front window of the old man's house. Webb laughed. It was a short guffaw, and it surprised him. He smiled as he drove back to town.

* * *

Webb sat on a chair while Mr. Baylor slipped a size ten Florsheim onto his foot. "That feel okay?"

Webb nodded. Baylor laced up the shoe.

"Go ahead."

Webb paced the store.

"Is it slippin'?"

"Nope."

"Wanna try the other?"

Baylor was older than Webb by twenty years. Webb wondered if he ever hurt the man or someone close to him, and then he remembered Baylor had a younger brother who worked at the mill, who he'd run-in with years earlier. He couldn't remember the details, but he recalled police involvement.

"This is a fine shoe," said Baylor. He laced up the other shoe. "I recommend protectant. In this weather you need it."

Webb wanted to say something, apologize for whatever he did to his brother. He didn't know if saying something might make it worse. "Thank you," he said. "And I'll take that protectant."

"I'm not trying to upsell you."

"No, I know. This rain wrecked my last pair."

"Okee-doke," said Baylor.

Webb walked up the hill in his new shoes. He watched the faces of the people he passed and tried to figure out how he could change all of their minds about him.

The nurse buzzed him in. She noticed his suit.

"I'm going out for dinner," he said. He walked down the hall, and then stopped. "Sarah, right? Are you still singing?" he asked.

The nurse smiled. "Oh Webb, I haven't sung in years."

"I remember that Christmas assembly. You sure had a pretty voice."

"That was a million years ago."

He walked to the end of the hall. George's door was open, but he knocked lightly before entering.

"I brought the receipts. Most of the fish is sold, so I called the fishery. They can deliver on the weekend."

"How's Pearl?"

"She misses you."

George looked out the window at an oak tree. Its bare branches trembled in the wind. "Give me my water," he said.

Webb took the glass from the table and lifted it to the old man's lips. He tipped it slightly, and George drank in loud gulps. He asked him who came to the store, but Webb knew what he meant.

"They were asking for you."

"What'dya say?"

"I told 'em you were hangin' tough."

Outside the room, a couple of nurses talked. Webb wanted to close the door and give George his privacy, but a moment later the voices trailed off. He placed the roll of receipts on the table next to the photo.

"I'll leave 'em for you," said Webb. He went to the door. "I don't steal," he said. "I never stole a cent from you."

George squeezed his eyes shut. "Nobody asked how I was doing, did they?"

Webb cleared his throat. "Course they did."

*   *   *

Webb stopped at the general store. He rang up a bouquet of mixed flowers and put ten dollars in the till. He locked the front door and walked down the hill to the Frontier.

81

Alice sat on the front lobby couch wearing a raincoat over her periwinkle dress. Milo's TV played quietly. Mitzi sat next to him, her head rested on his shoulder.

The front door opened and Webb entered, wearing his suit and carrying a small bouquet of flowers. She took the flowers and kissed him on the cheek.

Mitzi glanced over. "Let me put 'em in somethin' for you."

Alice gave the flowers to Mitzi.

"They'll be here when you get back."

The night was cold. Mist rose off the river. As they walked, Alice reached for his hand. She told him about how Jimmy fired her, and now it seemed funny.

He asked if she was going to stay in Waiden and she said she didn't know what she was going to do.

They walked in silence after that.

They entered the restaurant early. The hostess, a tall, graceful woman whom Alice recognized, led them to their table. Votive candles sat in clear glass over white tablecloths.

They were seated in a small room next to the main dining area.

Webb stopped the hostess. "Excuse me. I asked for a table by the window."

"Oh, I'm sorry. Those tables are reserved."

Webb gazed at the row of empty tables while the woman handed them menus and told them their waitress would be with them shortly.

When the waitress appeared, Alice recognized her, a pale girl who came in to Buffalo Burgers with her friends.

"Can I start you off with something to drink?"

"We reserved a window table," said Alice.

"Oh, I don't know," she said. "I can get the manager if you want."

"It's fine," said Webb.

The waitress disappeared. A moment later, the tall woman entered. "Is there something I can help you with?"

Webb cleared his throat. "I made a reservation for the window."

"I'm sorry, those tables are full for tonight."

"I called this morning."

"Really?" she said. "Whoever was working must not have written it down."

"You were working. It's Linda, right?"

The woman stiffened. "I'm sorry, but if you want to come back another time or during the week when we're not so busy . . ."

"During the week?" said Alice.

The woman smiled through her teeth. "Or whenever . . ."

"Okay," said Webb.

"I hope you enjoy your meal."

The waitress appeared behind Linda, smiling obliviously. Linda disappeared around the corner.

"Are we all set?"

"I'll have a glass of Merlot," said Alice.

"Just a water," said Webb.

The waitress went away.

"It's all right," said Alice. "I like it here. This is a nice spot."

They studied their menus. A couple entered and were seated by the window in the front room across from them. Alice noticed that the woman was Joyce. She watched as Joyce casually reached across the table and tapped her husband's arm. The man glanced over, and nodded slightly to his wife. Webb casually lifted his menu to cover his face.

Alice looked at Joyce and smiled. "Hi Joyce. How's the notions business?"

Joyce forced a smile. "Just fine, thank you."

Webb let the menu fall from his face as the waitress returned to take their orders.

They ordered their meals. They sat in awkward silence, waiting for the food to arrive.

Alice tried to think of something to say, but the more she searched for words, the more each comment seemed absurd.

"It's okay," she said. She reached her hand across the table.

He nodded stiffly.

Joyce glanced over at them. Alice stared directly at the woman. Joyce grimaced, her eyebrows shot upward. The waitress arrived and Joyce glanced toward Alice's table, "Looks like you're letting anyone in these days," she said.

"They're talking about us," said Alice to Webb.

Webb leveled Alice with a look. When Joyce glanced over again, she met Alice's gaze and shook her head pityingly.

"Is there a problem?" asked Alice loudly.

Webb said, "Stop it."

Joyce smirked. She made a *pfft* sound with her lips.

Alice was about to respond. Linda reentered the room, stood in the doorway and looked at them both.

"Let's go," said Webb.

"Why? Why should we leave?"

"We're going to go," Webb said to Linda.

"Well, it was nice having you."

Webb pushed back his chair and stood.

"You have a real problem," said Alice to Joyce.

"That's enough." Linda put a hand on Alice's shoulder.

"Don't touch me."

Joyce rolled her eyes. Her husband sat with his head turned, pretending to gaze down at the river.

Alice pushed her chair back and it fell over. She barged past Joyce. "I hope you get mercury poisoning."

Webb walked ahead of her. She followed him through the front door and outside.

He paced in a small circle on the path.

"Why did you leave?" she asked.

"I couldn't stay in there."

"They were talking about us," she said.

"They were talking about me."

"And I was sticking up for you."

"Why?"

"Because I care about you!"

"Well, stop it!" He walked away.

"What are you waiting for? Are you waiting for someone to forgive you? Cause it's not going to happen. No one is ever going to forgive you. Never. It's never going to happen. Do you realize that? Do you think if you're good enough for long enough then suddenly people are going to forget what you did? It doesn't work like that."

He stopped walking. "Then what do I do?"

"Stop waiting. Start living your life. You can't wait for people to forgive you. Life is too short."

"This is not the same as marrying the wrong person. What you did you can undo."

"It's not what you did that is killing you. It's your fear of everyone else. Don't you see—some people just need to have an enemy. Stop being that for them. You can't forgive yourself. Maybe you're not supposed to. Maybe you're just supposed to do something positive. Are you just going to hate yourself until they tell you it's enough?"

A flash of rage tore through him. She saw it pass across his eyes and she stepped back. He walked under a tree. "I can't do this," he said.

"I'm sorry," she said. "I see you holding on to this regret, like one day it's going to pay off."

He looked up, his eyes frozen in the moonlight. A couple passed them on their way into the restaurant. Alice recognized the woman's perfume, the same scent her mother wore, and for a moment she felt a rush of panic like everything was leaving her at once. She turned to see the woman's face, but she was gone.

Webb sat on a rock. He put his hands on his thighs and stared at the ground. Through the window he watched Joyce and her husband eating their appetizers. Something trembled in Alice underneath her skin. The forest was quiet. A bird's wings flapped above them. Water dripped from the trees. Webb gazed at the river, a slick serpent moving silently toward the ocean. "Just looking at you brings it all back."

"I'm cold," she said. "I'm going back to my room."

He watched her walk away. She hoped she would hear him behind her, but all she heard were frogs in the bulrushes and crickets in the leaves.

82

She emerged from the forest and crossed the street to the hotel. Two men sat on the couches in the lobby. She nodded at one of them, and he nodded back.

She walked down the hallway to her room. Ruth's door opened and Percy stepped out; his face was ruddy, a crimson rash at his throat. He leered. Alice stopped walking until he reached his door. He fished for his keys and she glanced into Ruth's room. Ruth sat on the floor with her left eye sealed shut by a mass of darkened flesh. A crusted line of congealed blood ran across it.

Alice charged at Percy, and as he turned she landed on him, pulling him down. His knees buckled. They fell to the floor, and she sat on top of him, pounding her fists into his face.

"He didn't do it," cried Ruth.

"I didn't do nothing!"

Percy held out his hands, covering his face.

But Alice couldn't stop. She was hitting him, screaming, "No, no, no, no." Ruth tried to pull her off him.

Percy threw a hand out weakly and caught Alice on the chin, but she couldn't feel anything until a tremendous force ripped her from him. Her breath left her. She fell to the floor and looked up to see Milo's small black eyes gazing down on her.

"She attacked me," said Percy.

"Get in your room," said Milo.

"You crazy bitch," said Percy, searching for his key on the floor. He snatched it up and shoved it into the lock. He disappeared inside.

Alice stood. She was about to say something to Milo, but he was already halfway down the hall.

"I'll sue you bitch," screamed Percy from inside his room.

"Can it, Percy," said Ruth.

Ruth pulled Alice into her room. A moment later there was a knock at the door. "You're dead," said Percy. Alice threw open the door, murder in her eyes. His mouth fell open and he slunk back to his room.

Alice sat on the bed while Ruth went to the mirror, examining the damage. "It was Doyle," said Ruth, dabbing at her eye with a wad of toilet paper. "I was on my break. Ricky just paid me, which he never does till I'm done for the night. I went out back for a smoke and Doyle came around with his buddies. They rolled me, and he took all my pay. Said it was payback for what I said at the diner." She hung her head. When she looked up, Alice saw her front tooth was missing.

"We're going to the police."

"No," said Ruth. "He'll just deny it. Besides, they won't hire me no more. That's what Ricky said."

"Ricky knows?"

"What do you think?! I bet he set me up. I bet Doyle gave him half his money back. Ricky says if I squeal, I can kiss my job goodbye."

"But you're not going back, are you?"

"What else am I going to do? We don't all come from Bellevue!" she shrieked, balling her hands into fists and shaking them at her sides.

"Okay. It's Okay."

"I was never no dominatrix," said Ruth. "I just made all that up cause I wanted to impress you. All I ever done is been a goddamn backwoods peeler."

Her body heaved.

Alice hugged her. She let her cry on her shoulder. Ruth's fingers dug into her back. Alice could feel Ruth's muscles twitching under her flesh, until gradually the tears abated and her body went limp.

"If I see Doyle again, I'm gonna stab his eyes out."

Alice stroked her head.

"I thought we were gonna be friends."

"We are friends. We just had an argument, that's all."

"Nobody ever took me to the ocean before," she said. "Every guy I ever been with was a goddamn Doyle. I didn't tell you about Webb cause I knew you'd freak out. He's a good guy."

"Shhh." Alice glanced at the crumpled singles on Ruth's table. "What was Percy doing here?"

"I needed bus fare."

Alice took a breath, and for a moment she feared she might be sick.

"I gotta lie down," said Ruth. She lay on the bed. "My feet are cold."

"Do you want some socks?"

"Yeah. They're in the drawer."

Alice opened the drawer and found a pair of men's woolen socks. She pulled them onto Ruth's feet, then climbed onto the bed next to her.

"Whenever I go to Portland, I go to the Lloyd Mall, and there's this lady who sells jewelry from a cart outside. She's the one who said I could make my own bracelets. Do you think anyone'd buy jewelry from me?"

"Of course they would."

"You're not just saying that?"

"Honey, with your personality, the sky's the limit."

Ruth sniffled. "That's probably true."

She climbed back out of bed and lit a joint. She handed it to Alice.

Alice rolled off the bed. "I better go to sleep." She went to the door. "You wanna get some breakfast tomorrow?"

Ruth sucked hard on the joint and pursed her lips, then blasted out a cloud of smoke.

"Try me in the morning."

83

Webb sat on the rock until he was sure Alice was gone. Then he stood and headed back. The air was cold, but his adrenaline kept him warm. He walked fast until he slipped and fell in the darkness, cutting his hand on a rock. He turned and headed back. He walked along the path, playing over in his head everything she had said. As he passed the front door of the Frontier his pace quickened.

He went up to his room and opened the fridge. He made a sandwich. He ate it and stared down at the Pastime. He prayed while he ate, asked God for an answer. He removed the empty scotch bottle from the trash. The urge thrummed in his belly. He carried it down the back stairs to the alley and threw it in the bin.

84

Webb lay in bed staring at his clock. He couldn't sleep. At five a.m. he rolled out of bed and took a shower. He got dressed and went outside.

It was still dark when he entered the hospital. The nurse stood behind the glass. "We called you at the store. Didn't have your number."

She led him to George's room. He stared at the empty bed, the crisp white sheets wrapped tightly under the mattress where George used to be. The photograph was still on the side table. Webb reached for it. A white envelope sat next to it, Webb's name written on the front. The nurse's face was tight. She explained how she went to check on George during the night, and that his breathing had stopped. They tried to revive him, but he bled into his brain. Webb shoved the photograph into his pocket. In the distance he could hear the wail of an ambulance. Out the window he watched flashing red lights scrape the rooftops. The ambulance appeared at the crest of the hill. He stuffed the envelope into his pocket and followed the nurse into the hallway.

In the lobby a paramedic and orderly hopped out of the ambulance and opened the back door. They pulled a man out on a gurney. Webb held the front door open for them. Ned Feeney's scarred face looked up at Webb from the stretcher. Blood soaked through the white sheet where he bled from his belly. His face was as relaxed as a child. From where Webb stood it looked like Ned Feeney was smiling at him. "I got him," said Ned, as they rolled him past.

85

Alice helped Ruth wash up, and then she applied makeup to disguise the damage. Ruth's eye was swollen shut; a thin line of congealed blood ran from the top of her eyebrow in a vertical line over the lid like a zipper. They filled a garbage bag with a stack of Styrofoam take-out boxes and loose trash from her room, and then Ruth opened her trunk and filled a second bag with its contents. They took the trash out the side door of the hotel and tossed it into the dumpster.

They walked up the street to Mitzi's and examined the sunglasses. They each picked a pair while a man with a cast over his right hand hammered out a deal with Mitzi over his fishing pole. He explained how he lost his thumb on a separating machine at the mill the previous week, and was in need of a left-handed pole. "C'mon Mitzi, this here's a Tidal Flat."

Ten bucks is what I can do," she said. Now let me help these ladies."

Alice paid Mitzi two dollars, and then she and Ruth walked into the drizzle with their sunglasses on.

86

Webb sat across from Jane Tripp in her office. Her German Shepherd stared at Webb through half-opened eyes. Webb stared back, avoiding Tripp's scrutiny.

"Mr. Cooley, did you hear what I said?"

"Yes, ma'am."

"Do you have a response?"

He shook his head. "Nope."

"The hearings officer is not going to give you a second warning. If you break parole again, they assure me, they *will* send you back."

The animal sat on its haunches, fur bristled along its spine. Webb shifted in his chair. Sometimes he prayed when he sat there, asked God for evenness of mind.

"Mr. Cooley, I'm not sure you understand what I'm saying."

He stared at her, unmoved. The dog bared its teeth and began a low growl.

"If you leave the city limits within the next two years, you face another stint," she said. "Life has consequences. Do you understand?"

He remained motionless.

She placed her pen on the desk and looked into his eyes.

"I want to go back," he said.

"Excuse me?" There was a flicker at the edge of her mouth. "You're having a bad day," she said.

"No." He stared at his new shoes. "They're all the same," he said. "I can't do it. I'm not cut out for this. I reckon I never was."

The dog settled back and closed its eyes.

"Mr. Cooley that may be the most honest thing I've ever heard."

"I'm not happy about it."

"Are you concerned you might harm someone?"

He stared at the floor. "No, ma'am."

"Are you concerned you might harm yourself?"

His eyes were wet. "No."

She watched him, studied his body language. "I'm sorry, Mr. Cooley," she said. And then she laughed, a hiccup, then gulped it back down. "Well, if this isn't the darndest conversation," she said. She signed her name at the bottom of the report and slid it across the desk. "I'm afraid I cannot recommend incarceration at this time."

87

Webb walked through the parking lot. He passed the police station. He glanced in the window and saw John sitting at his desk. John waved and went back to work on his computer.

Webb rounded the corner of the bank, and walked up the hill. He stood outside the store, stared in the front window at the sign that read CLOSED, and wondered if he still had a job. He turned to go back to his apartment when he heard a voice.

"What are you staring at?" The kid stood a few feet up the hill with a hand on his hip. "Ain't you gonna open it?"

"Don't you have school today?"

"Not on Saturday." The kid looked like he was ready for a fight.

Webb shoved his key in and opened the door. He let the kid inside.

"What's your name, anyway?"

"Trevor."

"I'm Webb." Webb shoved out his hand. They shook.

"I know your name."

"Don't matter. It's good manners."

Trevor looked at Webb, staring into his eyes. "You don't seem like you done what you did."

"Thank you." Webb patted the boy on the shoulder. "I guess our past don't have to follow us," he said. He looked the kid up and down. Trevor wore the same clothes from days earlier. His hair was greasy, and he had an odor.

"So, what do you want me to do?"

Webb fished the key from his pocket. "I need a right-hand man."

"For what?"

"Everything. Cleaning up, stocking shelves, bagging groceries . . . what do you think?"

He scratched his forehead with his thumb. "I don't know," he said. "I guess so."

"Well then, let's get to it."

He walked the kid to the back of the store, filled a bucket with hot water and soap, and showed him how to mop.

"Where do you live, anyway?" asked Webb.

"Over on Tremaine. We moved here last year from Powers. My daddy works with my uncle at the mill."

"Does he know you ditch school?"

"He don't care."

"I doubt that," said Webb. "But anyway, if you're working for me, I care. I can't have a truant working here. It's bad for business." Webb didn't know what made him do it, but he tore off a sheet of butcher paper and grabbed a pen from the register. "I need you to sign a contract before you start."

"Contract?"

"Says as long as you work here, you won't ditch school or steal from no one, and you'll be a generally cheerful person."

"I'm not signing no contract."

"Then I'll leave you to the police to sort out this shoplifting business."

Webb wrote the date at the top of the paper along with a sentence saying he agreed to not ditch school or shoplift and to be of general good cheer. He handed the pen to Trevor to read over. The boy pursed his lips. "I said I'm not signing nothing."

"Son, can you write your name?"

"No, sir."

"You never have to be ashamed of not being able to do something. I'm gonna teach you how to print your name. All right?"

"Yes, sir."

* * *

Later that morning, Webb stood behind the register and removed the photograph of George and his bride from his pocket. He took some masking tape from the drawer and taped the picture to the front of the register. On the tape he wrote:

George Plotki died today.
He will be missed by those who knew him.

* * *

Mrs. Packer entered the store. She shuffled up the aisle and grabbed a box of Stillmans off the shelf. Trevor was in the back room chopping the heads off carrots. Whack. Whack. Whack. Webb watched the old woman make her way toward him at the register.

"Good morning, Mrs. Packer."

The woman looked at Webb. She turned back to see if George was following behind her.

Webb stepped back from the counter. The old woman looked down the aisle and coughed, waiting for George. And then her eyes fell to the photograph on the register. She studied it. Her eyes blinked rapidly. She made a sound with her teeth. "For heaven's sake."

She lifted her chin, which meant for Webb to ring her up. He punched in the price on the register and put her cookies in a bag. She paid him, then looked up and smiled, a tight little smile. "Have a nice day, Mr. Cooley."

"You too, Mrs. Packer."

She shuffled to the door and climbed into her car.

88

A lice and Ruth sat in the back booth of Corky's. They wore dark sunglasses. Ruth sucked on the last of her vanilla milkshake. "That's about all I'm gonna miss of this town."

"What about me?"

"You're leaving too, ain't you?"

"I guess I am," said Alice.

"What happened?"

"I don't know."

Alice's face flushed—her pale skin had a marbled look like she was near tears. "I guess we'll be friends."

"That sounds like bullshit. What does that mean?"

"It means it didn't work out." She gazed out the window at the Frontier.

"What are you going to do?"

"Go back to San Francisco. Start painting again."

Ruth reached for her purse.

"I got it," said Alice. She laid a ten-dollar bill on the table.

Ruth picked up her cardboard trunk at the door.

"Hold on a second," said Alice. She stopped the waitress and handed her a ten-dollar bill. "I need lots of change." The waitress handed her a roll of quarters.

They walked outside. Alice opened her bag and handed Ruth a thick envelope.

"No. What's this? What are you doing?"

"It's just a little something to keep you going for a bit."

"Nah, come on. What are you doing?"

"Just take it."

"What are you doing?" Ruth stared at the envelope.

"And if you need anything, you call me, all right? I wrote my cell number in there. Just give me a coupla days to get a new phone."

They walked down the hill together, then Ruth stopped. "Am I ever going to see you again?"

"I don't know. I sure hope so."

Ruth put her trunk down and wrapped her arms around Alice. "I think I'm gonna get the bus on my own."

"I want to walk with you."

"Don't make me cry, woman. My mama was married six times. I'm not good with goodbyes. Don't promise me anything. I'd rather you say you had no plans on ever seeing me again, and then surprised me."

"All right. I got no plans on seeing you again."

"That's better." She slapped Alice on the shoulder. "Don't take shit from people." She picked up her trunk and lumbered down the sidewalk to the bus stop.

The Greyhound rolled past at the bottom of the street. Ruth walked to the end of the block and disappeared around the corner. Alice waited for a few minutes, until she heard the gasp of the hydraulic door, and the high rev of the motor as the bus pulled away.

89

Lester entered the general store and approached Webb at the counter. He pulled a packet of gum from the rack and unwrapped a stick. He glanced at the photograph on the cash register. "Sorry to hear about your boss," he said. He shoved the gum into his mouth. "I know you two were real close." He twirled the wrapper between his fingers.

"Can I help you with something?"

Lester tilted his head. "You're kidding me, right?" He looked at Webb for a moment. "You've been to the hospital, right?"

Webb nodded.

Lester's eye widened. "They didn't give you the papers?"

Webb wiped his hands on his apron and reached into his back pocket. He removed the envelope. He opened it to find a four-page document. In bold type at the top of the page, it read, *PLOTKI ESTATE.* Following the words, *I hereby bequeath to . . .* Webb saw his name.

Lester twirled the gum wrapper around in circles until it

snapped. "He called me yesterday to draw it up." He tossed the wrapper on the counter. "This don't make you respectable," he said. "People like you don't know how to keep shit anyway." He smiled through his teeth. "This place'll be worth nothin' in a coupla years."

Lester walked to the door.

"Hey," said the kid.

Lester turned.

The kid joined Webb behind the counter. "You didn't pay for the gum."

Lester smirked. He looked at Webb. "Is he joking?"

The kid looked at Webb.

Webb shook his head. "It's fifty cents."

Lester's eyes crinkled at the edges. He walked back to the register, opened his wallet and tossed a dollar bill on the counter. Webb showed the kid the button to open the till. The kid took the dollar bill, smoothed it on the counter and placed it into the register. Webb showed him the roll of quarters wrapped in paper. The kid began slowly to peel the paper. Lester stood waiting. He grew impatient. "Ah, keep the goddamn change."

90

Alice rolled her suitcase down the hallway. She stopped in the lobby and said goodbye to Milo. She asked if she could get some rent back for leaving mid-week. He stared and shook his head. On her way out the door, she stopped at the payphone. She took a breath and dialed her mother. The automated voice asked for three dollars. She shoved twelve quarters into the slot.

"Alice? Don't hang up."

"I'm not hanging up, Mom."

"I keep calling you. I've called you a million times."

"I told you my phone was broken."

"What else could I do?" Her mother was crying.

"Mom, I'm so sorry."

"Please don't hang up. I won't survive. You have no idea how much this hurts me."

"I'm not going to hang up."

"You promise?"

"I promise."

"I don't understand you. Honestly, I don't know what you're afraid of. It's like you think we've got some kind of magical power over you. Have we ever stopped you from doing anything?"

"No, mom. You haven't."

"And you've always done whatever you wanted."

"I know. You're right. I thought I was afraid of you making me do something. But I was afraid of me."

"Honestly, Alice. I don't understand half of what you say."

"I've never wanted to let you down."

"You're not still involved with that man, are you?"

"No."

"You can't just quit when the going gets tough. Chick is a good man. He loves you."

"Mom, we're going to have different opinions about this, but I'm afraid mine is sort of the only one that matters. And I felt like marrying him was quitting."

"For God sakes, you had a great life with him."

"Did I?"

"You had security."

It was the way her mother said the word *security*—she sounded furious with Alice, as if something in her was being threatened, as if Alice's decision challenged every choice Trish had ever made.

"But Mom," she said. "I never felt secure."

"That's because we spoiled you. What are you going to do?" She could hear the hysteria in her mother's voice.

"I don't know."

"Sweetheart, you have no skills. You're going to be forty."

"I'm an artist. That's a skill. And I'm going to be thirty-eight."

"You can't just walk out on someone."

"Do you want me to be happy, Mom?"

"What kind of question is that?"

"Well, I am. For the first time in my life."

"But what are you going to do?"

"I don't know."

"Your generation doesn't understand commitment. You have no respect for marriage. You probably figure you can just live off his alimony."

"Actually, I signed a prenup."

"Alice, this is not the time to make jokes. You have no idea how tough it is out there." Trish was crying. "I love you, but you have to grow up. You can't keep living in this fantasy world."

"Mom, I'll call you when I get back to San Francisco."

"Where are you going to live?"

"I'll work it out."

"But you have no plan."

"I guess I'm gonna trust God."

"You're making fun of me."

"I'm sorry. I'm just teasing you." Alice gazed out the window. "I'll come up soon, okay?"

"What happened with the felon?"

"I better get on the road."

"Call me when you're in San Francisco."

"I will."

"You promise?"

"I promise."

"We'll send you some money."

"Bye, Mom."

91

She walked out to the parking lot dragging her suitcase. The rain had stopped. The river was swollen and spilling over the edges. Her eyes tracked the path where she had disappeared into the forest with Webb and she felt her stomach grab. Her car was backed up against the sidewalk. She lifted the suitcase into the trunk. At the bottom of the hill, Lester rounded the corner. He was smoking a cigarette and talking to himself.

"You okay?" she asked.

He laughed wryly, looking at the cigarette between his fingers.

"It's a bitch," she said.

"Minor setback," he said. "So, you heading home?"

"Looks that way."

"If you're up again, give me a call." He smiled, but he looked lost.

"You sure you're all right?"

He scratched his head, and then put the cigarette to his lips and took a quick drag. "Our buddy just had a little windfall," he said. He pointed at the general store. "I don't know if you heard, but George died."

"Oh my gosh."

"Yeah," said Lester. "Left him the business."

"No."

He cleared his throat. "Left him everything. His *house* . . ." he kept nodding. "Everything."

Alice gazed at the general store and grinned. Lester shook his head in amazement.

"Hang in there," she said.

She climbed into her car. As she drove up the hill, Lester was still standing on the sidewalk, watching her drive off, cigarette in his mouth.

When she reached the top of the hill, she pulled her car over to the curb. She got out and walked down the hill to Secondhand Treasures.

"How much do you want for that fishing rod?" she asked Mitzi.

"This is one of them Tidal Flat series. Very rare. I couldn't give it to you for less than sixty-five."

Alice opened her purse, but there was not enough money. Reaching further into her bag, she removed her wedding ring from the bottom and placed it on the counter. "Can you still give me seventy-five for it?"

Mitzi studied the ring. "You sure about this?"

"Positive."

92

Webb held the stepladder with one hand while the kid handed him gallon cans of apple juice. Balancing the cans on his palm, Webb placed them on a lower shelf.

"How come you're moving these?"

"They're too high. They could land on someone's head."

He was showing the kid how to work the register when she walked into the store carrying a fishing rod. He placed a hand on the boy's shoulder. "Go back and finish mopping."

The kid looked at Alice, and retreated to the stock room.

"You got some help," she said.

He shrugged. "You gonna be okay?"

"I'm going to be fine."

"You'll be better than that," he said. He shifted some mints on the counter. "Why don't you take some lunch for the road?" He reached into the cooler and removed a sandwich.

"No. Thank you. I just wanted to say goodbye." She placed the fishing rod on the counter. "I heard about George. I thought you could use this."

He stared at the rod like it was a hand grenade. He scratched his cheek. The room was cool, but beads of sweat formed at his temple and he pushed them away with an open palm. "For what?"

"You told me you could leave the city limits for work."

He tried to hand the rod back to her, but she dropped her hands at her sides, so he placed it on the counter. The kid peeked out from behind the stock room door. Webb stared at the rod.

"If you don't want it, you can take it back to Mitzi," she said. She reached across the counter and squeezed his hand, then turned and left.

93

A lice walked up the hill and climbed into her car.

She rounded the corner and glanced across the street to see Trudy standing in front of *Notions and Appliances*, arms squeezed around herself, shivering from the cold. When Trudy saw Alice she turned away, pretending not to see her, and suddenly Alice knew who had told Joyce about her breakfasts with Ruth. She was struck by Trudy's loyalty, the slavish devotion to her captor. Trudy was no different than everybody else. She was obedient to the familiar.

Alice rounded the bend of towering firs. She thought about her obedience to Chick, or at least to whom she had spent her marriage believing him to be. Those days were gone, and she never had to waste another moment attempting to rewrite them. As she approached the overpass, she slowed her car. She signaled left and turned onto the ramp heading south. She pressed on the gas pedal, merging with the light morning traffic. The sky was clear and the forest to her right exploded in ochre, russet, and crimson. The road angled to the west, and as she reached a promontory, the sea came into view. She lowered her window and stuck her arm into the wind to feel the day.

As she drove, she heard the sound of a truck horn behind her. In her rearview mirror, she saw Webb sitting high in his seat. He drove alongside her, shouting for her to pull over. "I want to talk to you," he said. His eyes were fierce and shining.

She hit her signal and slowed her car to the side. He jumped out of the truck and she watched in her rearview as he approached. He wore the red-checkered fishing jacket that she had seen George wear. It fit tightly over his hard shoulders.

"I just wanted to say thank you," he said.

"You mean, for the rod?" she asked, with a smile.

"For everything," he said.

A logging truck roared past them and he pushed himself close to her window to keep the dust from flying into her face.

"I was wondering if maybe you'd still like to see that rock?" he said.

She watched the logging truck retreat into the distance.

"It's just a ways back," he said. "I can drive you, and bring you back."

"Will my car be okay here?"

"I reckon. Just pull it over some more."

She parked her car and climbed out. He stood at the back of her car, holding his hand over his eyes like a visor. His face was still, and as she walked toward him, she felt suddenly shy. "Is it okay for you to be out here?"

"I gotta get the fish," he said. He smiled crookedly. "Part of my job."

He opened the passenger door of the truck and she climbed

in. He waited for some cars to pass before doing a U-turn and heading back up the highway.

He pulled onto the shoulder and they climbed out of the truck.

She followed behind him as they walked down a narrow path into the woods.

"It's just past these trees," he said.

She remembered the first time she looked at his drawings and how he stood behind her and she could feel him. She remembered the warmth that flooded her body.

The only sound was their feet shuffling through a blanket of fallen leaves.

A slippery, moss covered log lay across their path. Webb reached for her hand and helped her over it. A cottontail darted across the path and stopped for a moment, lifting its ears back, and then vanished under a fern.

Ahead they came to a clearing and the sun appeared. They entered a meadow. Gophers stood like miniature sentinels, their heads poking above the grass, heads moving in short, quick movements.

They followed the winding path as it led down a steep, craggy cliff. Webb held her hand and together they walked down to a beach of round white rocks.

"It's just around this rock," he said.

Alice smiled. She didn't speak. As they rounded the cliff she saw it in the distance, a slick black rock jutting into the surf like the back of a giant serpent. The waves smashed against it with only its top surface remaining dry. It was precisely as he had sketched it, and yet, somehow it looked different, like nothing she could have imagined. She suddenly realized that a part of her did not believe it existed.

"Let's go," she said, squeezing his hand. "Let's walk on it."

"The waves can get pretty high," he said. "You're gonna get wet."

"It's just water," she said, and together they walked toward the rock.

THE END

ACKNOWLEDGEMENTS

It took fourteen years to write this little book. I had to get married, have a kid, and get over myself (an ongoing project.) I want to thank my assistant, Katharine Wilson, who happens to be one of the best editors I know. I appreciate all of your hard work. Thank you to my agent, Matthew Snyder, at Creative Artists for sticking with me. You are a very classy gentleman. Thank you to the good people of Gold Beach, Oregon, whose names now escape me because it took so damn long to write this thing I've misplaced all of your names. Needless to say you were very helpful in showing me your jail, explaining the Oregon parole process, and answering all my questions from the wholesale price of chanterelle mushrooms to details on salmon fishing limits. Lastly, I want to thank my wife, Mary-Beth, and my son, Ray. This book would not exist without you.